S0-BYN-370

FIX HER UP

Carey Heywood
New York Times Bestselling Author

FIX HER UP
Copyright © Carey Heywood LLC
All right reserved.

Editor: Jennifer Van Wyk
Cover design: Hang Le
Paperback formatting: Integrity Formatting

Except as permitted under the U.S. Copyright Act of 1976, no part of this publication may be reproduced, distributed, or transmitted in any form or by any means, or stored in a database or retrieval system, without prior written permission of the author.

The scanning, uploading, and distribution of this book via the Internet or via other means without the permission of the publisher are illegal and the punishable by law. Please purchase only authorized electronic editions and do not participate in or encourage electronic piracy of copyrighted materials. Your support of the author's rights is appreciated.

Fix Her Up is a work of fiction. Names, characters, places, and incidents either are the product of the author's imagination or are used fictitiously. Any resemblance to actual persons, living or dead, events, or locales is entirely coincidental.

Visit my website at www.careyheywood.com

DEDICATION

To anyone who thinks they are a fixer upper,
I think you're move-in ready.

CHAPTER 1

Finley

EVERY ADVENTURE HAS a beginning. I assumed mine would be more glamorous than fishing around my glove compartment for something to blow my nose with. This is the real world though, and viruses could give a crap.

Success! A napkin!

The relief that comes from blowing my nose is short lived. The leaky faucet that has taken up residence front and center on my face does nothing but drip, drip, and drip some more.

My brakes make an embarrassing screech as I pull into a drug store parking lot, narrowly missing a truck.

Finley Reeves, you need to get your shit together.

And while you're at it, stop referring to yourself in the third person.

The truck successfully avoids me and I lift my hand in a lame apology. It'd be just my luck to get into a car accident this close to the end of my journey. Driving cross-country with the head cold from hell has zapped all my energy. If I didn't need medicine to kill whatever it is I've got, I'd already be at my new house.

I park toward the back of the lot to leave room for the trailer packed full of all my earthly possessions hooked to the back of my car.

Grabbing a cart from the entrance, I zombie walk to the medicine aisle and load it full of store brand meds and tissue. On the way to the register, I pause to add a bottle of cheap wine. Sure, I'd rather celebrate with some fancy champagne or something like that. Unfortunately, for the time being, with all of my savings going to buy my house and now to fix it up, spending five bucks on wine is more in my budget.

When I turn back to the register, I'm annoyed to see the guy I almost hit in the parking lot has beat me to it. If I hadn't stopped for booze, I'd be on my way by now.

Instead, I'm waiting behind a guy buying . . . I lean to one side to see what he set next to the register then force back a groan. He's buying condoms, two boxes of them.

That's just perfect.

It's not just perfect; it's fucking poetic considering why I'm in this predicament. My eyes move to the clerk and I see her attention is fully focused on the guy in front of me. I squint, is she actually drooling? If she offers to help him use all those condoms I'll be forced to guzzle this bottle of wine right here, right now. That, or knock myself out with the bottle.

My inspection of her is interrupted when I feel a massive sneeze brewing.

"I'm opening these now," I mumble, reaching into my cart and grabbing a box of tissues. "I swear I'll pay," I mutter loud enough for the cashier to hear, before loudly blowing my nose.

The condom guy turns to stare with piercing blue

eyes.

I frown up at him. He unfortunately looks like someone who *should* be buying lots of condoms. Tall, I'd guess at least six foot, big broad shoulders, framing his athletic build. He's the All-American dream man with thick light brown hair, just the right amount of facial and a fantastic ass. In fact, he's almost too perfect. Are hallucinations a side effect of a head cold?

When he doesn't start ripping off all of his clothes, I decide he must be real.

"Do you mind?" I grumble.

"Feel better," he replies, and then turns back to the register to take his bag.

"Thanks," I mutter.

The clerk working the register regards my purchases with understanding. "Head cold?"

I give her a pitiful nod.

"Can I see your ID?" She asks.

Head cold or no head cold, I'm still flattered so I don't argue that I'm thirty-five as I dig it out.

"So, Finley Wiltshire, what are you doing in New Hampshire?"

"It's Reeves, not Wiltshire," I correct.

A wrinkle forms between her eyebrows as she points to my license. "It says Wiltshire."

My shoulders sag as I shove my used tissue into my pocket. "I just got divorced and haven't changed it back yet."

"Ahh, sorry," she mutters, handing it back to me.

"Yep," I reply bitterly, suddenly in the mood to share. "My ex got a girlfriend and a sports car while I got bronchitis. Sounds fair, right?"

She lets out a shocked laugh and then offers, "We also carry soup."

"Is it laced with whiskey?" I joke.

Blinking at me, she doesn't reply and I must be susceptible to suggestion because soup doesn't sound bad.

"I'll hold your stuff here if you want to grab a couple cans," she says.

With a longing, I glance over my shoulder to where their grocery type aisles are. Why are they so far away? It's embarrassing how tired and crappy I feel.

The clerk takes pity on me. "I'll grab it for you. Do you want one can or two?"

I try to smile but the longer I stand, the worse I feel.

My face hurts, pain radiating from my cheeks to my eye sockets. "Chicken Noodle. Two if you have it."

She gives the counter a rap with her knuckle before saying, "I'll be right back."

She comes back with two cans of soup and a can of ginger ale. "The ginger ale is on the house. It's made by a local company and you'll need something to take all your medicine with."

"Thank you," I murmur, grateful, but feeling guilty for assuming she was drooling over condom guy, maybe she's just nice.

It doesn't take long to pay for my things. Once I'm back in my car I open the cold meds first and wash a dose down with my free ginger ale.

I lift the can to study the label. Woodlake Ales. That clerk wasn't joking about it being local. Since this is Woodlake, New Hampshire, my new home.

All right, it's time for me to go home.

It was sold as is. The price was a steal, or highway

robbery depending on who you asked. Where every other buyer saw the broken, falling down mess of a house, I saw nothing but potential. I've spent the last decade having every decision I made criticized. Here, sink or swim, there will be no one second guessing me.

It's my fresh start.

Now I get to explore the space I've memorized from the pictures I clicked online.

It's an old Federal style house, its worn siding a sad gray. Seems perfect for me since I'm a bit worn and sad myself.

The symmetry of the exterior is what called to me, that and all the windows. I can already imagine how light and airy it will be someday.

If I can do this, fix up this old house, I'll be giving the both of us a new lease on life.

My parents are convinced it's going to be a money pit but I don't care. It's all mine. I'm going to fix it up bit by bit even if it takes me a decade to do it.

It wiped out a good chunk of my renovation budget, but I had the place rewired right after I closed on it. It was the only way I could convince my parents I wasn't going to die in an electrical fire.

Soon the cable company is coming to get my internet hooked up. The company I work for approved me to work remotely as long as I have internet.

Once I found out I could work anywhere, I decided it was time to make a move. My only requirement for my new home was it had to be a house I could buy outright and fix up someplace far, far away.

Woodlake, New Hampshire was about as far away from Springfield, Texas as I could manage.

My new to me place has a long drive on the right side,

long enough to park my car and the trailer I'm pulling, without it hanging over the sidewalk.

This place has almost no yard, being the last house on a dead end. I used Google maps to check out the other houses on the block before I bought it, which are in much better condition.

My hope, and what I talked my parents into was because of that, this will be a safe place to live. Not that I needed their permission, I'm thirty-five years old. I have a great job.

My parents are under the impression that I'm having a mid-life crisis of some sort. I always thought that was reserved for men who suddenly get divorced, buy a sports car and start dating women half their age, pretty much what my ex-husband, Allen, did.

I got our old house in the divorce. It was our negotiation as long as I didn't pursue alimony.

He didn't want me anymore, so I don't want his money. Me, I just wanted something new, something that wasn't tainted by memories of him. They think I might be a little crazy for making this move but they love me so they're trying to be as supportive as they can.

I kill the ignition and grab my purse before I climb out. The afternoon sun caresses my skin, so different here than this time of day back in Texas. With a press to my key fob, I lock the doors and make my way to my front porch.

My new yard, small as it is, is completely overgrown. The stone path from the driveway is hard to navigate, with weeds as high as my knees on either side. There's another entrance at the end of the drive that leads directly into the kitchen.

With luck, that one will be in better shape. Since I drove from Texas and wasn't sure when I'd get here, the realtor left me the key in a lockbox attached to a door. I assumed it would be on the front one. After fighting through all the weeds, I learn the hard way she must have attached it to the kitchen door.

Groaning, I make my way back to the drive and then to the other entrance. When I get there, I'm relieved to see the box and use the combination she texted me to open it. Inside it, there's not one key, but four, all labeled: Front, Kitchen, Back and Shed.

Using the key labeled Kitchen, I let myself in. The first thing that hits me is the musty smell. It's a mixture of wet and mothballs and not even remotely pleasant.

There's a window over the sink. I try to open it. Ugh, painted shut. I move farther into my new house and try a window in the den. The same is true for it.

I wave the air in front of my nose.

Seriously, as congested as I am, I can't imagine how bad this place smells normally. Going from room to room, I manage to open windows in the living room, the dining room and the back door.

Thankfully, the fresh air helps with the smell. Hoping that the smell isn't an indication of the state of the house, I slowly turn, looking around the dingy room and let out a pitiful groan at the sight before me.

It's not just bad, it's BAD.

What the hell have I gotten myself into?

Doors hang from their hinges, and the floor creaks ominously with each step I take.

Before I bought the house, I had an inspection done, even though I knew I was getting it as is. The foundation was good and I took that as a sign that this house was the right one for me.

Sure, just about everything else in this house needs to

be restored or replaced. Someone stopped caring about this place a long time ago, and that's something I can relate to.

I walk back out to my car. I can unpack my trailer tomorrow so I can drop it off at a local U-Haul place. For now, I have enough stuff to camp out on the first floor. I grab my backpack and a duffle bag from the backseat.

The little bit of furniture I have I'm not unloading tonight. The exception to this is what's in my duffle, and a queen size air mattress. I plug it in so it can start filling. It's going to be my bed, sofa, and most of my other furniture for the time being.

Setting both on the floor inside the kitchen door, I turn around to get one more thing from the trunk of my car, my microwave.

I sneeze twice from my car to the kitchen door, each time clutching my microwave to my chest to avoid dropping it.

Once I have it inside I set it on countertop closest to the door and plug it in.

Then I stick my hand out the door and relock my car.

Pulling my phone from my pocket, I walk to the living room as it rings. My mom answers right away.

"Hey Finley," she greets.

"Hi Mama," I reply.

"Honey, have you taken any medicine? You sound like hell."

My nose starts stinging and it's not from an impending sneeze. "It's just a cold, Mom. It sounds way worse than it feels." I hope she can't tell I'm lying over the phone so I keep talking. "I stopped to get more medicine and soup."

"Make sure you drink lots of fluids. It will flush that

cold right out of you," she presses.

Fluids are my mom's cure for everything. She is as anti-dehydration as it gets. Her words remind me of the ginger ale I left sitting in the cup holder of my car. Heading for the door, I grab my keys. If I don't get it now I'll forget about it. If I forget about it and have to throw it away because it got all gross and stale, I'll feel guilty for wasting it.

"Are you walking around?" My mom asks.

"Yeah, I was sitting all day in the car and I forgot my drink in it. I'm trying to be a good girl and stay hydrated."

It's weird but after only a few times moving in and out of the kitchen door it already feels familiar. When I come back through it, ginger ale in hand, I give the door an extra hard tug. This saves me from having to yank on it twice to close it.

"Don't forget that case of bottled water we got you from the bulk store." My mom, the Queen of subtle reminders.

"It's in the trailer. I'll unpack it tomorrow," I promise.

She pauses, which I'm guessing means she's holding back from telling me to get the water right now. Instead, she says, "So, how is the house? Your daddy and I can't wait to fly out and see it. Have you changed your mind about making us wait?"

"Mom," I groan.

"Alright, alright. Just pretend I didn't bring it up, okay?"

Here comes the guilt.

"It's just that my baby girl is now thousands of miles away and it has been years, *years,* since I haven't seen you at least once a week. I know this is what you need to do. I'm just going to miss you."

"Mom." This time it's not a groan but a whisper.

This is the only part I hate about moving away. I love my family. My parents and I are close and have always been. My leaving Springfield had nothing to do with them and everything to do with me.

"Your dad is pestering me for the phone so I'm going to put him on now. I love you baby."

"I love you too, Mom," I sniffle, balling the hand not holding my phone into a fist, the bite of my nails into my palm keeping my tears at bay.

"Hey Finny. How was the drive? Did you hit any traffic?"

God, I love my dad. He is, and will always be obsessed with road conditions. He about had a coronary when I told them I was moving to New Hampshire and pretty much forbade me from attempting to drive in the snow.

"It wasn't too bad, Dad," I chuckle.

"You still sound all stuffy. You taking anything for it?"

I roll my eyes but I do it with a smile. "It's just a cold, Dad. Don't worry."

"Never going to happen," he replies and damn it my nose starts stinging again.

"How's your weekend going?" I change the subject, not wanting to cry.

"Everyday is a weekend for me," he jokes.

Ever since he retired that's been his favorite joke to tell.

"Hey, is it cold up there?"

I shake my head and start to imagine what color curtains would look good in here. "Dad, it's close to eighty today. It won't get super cold until winter."

Before he can bring up the snow and all of his

10

concerns surrounding it, I ask, "Did you and mom do anything fun today?"

"Yeah, we went to see that movie Clint Eastwood directed. It made her cry but it was a damn good movie."

"I'll keep an eye out for it. But hey, I think my mattress is full and it's been a long day. I'm going to make my soup and then crash. Is it okay if we talk more tomorrow?"

He pulls in a breath. "Of course darling. You eat your soup and get a good night of sleep. You'll feel better in the morning."

"Thanks Dad. I love you and give Mom a hug from me and tell her I love her too." My words come out in a rush, hoping they don't hear the emotion behind them.

"Okay Finny. I will. I love you too. You call us whenever you want," he says quietly.

I hate how sad he sounds. I can hear how much they miss me and it hits me harder than I expected it to.

"I promise I'll call, Dad."

After the call ends, I stare at my phone until the image assigned to their contact fades away as the screen dims. It's a picture of the two of them, at one of their many barbeques. Ten or so years ago my dad had a pool put in the backyard and their house has been party central ever since.

My mom has two sisters who also live in or near Springfield. My aunt Jane is divorced but her divorce didn't happen until my cousin Heather was in tenth grade. My aunt Charlotte is still married. They all love to come hang out by the pool while my dad mans the grill.

It's going to be weird knowing they're all there, without me. I taught my mom how to video chat with her cell before I left, but it won't be the same.

For the first time, my certainty in needing to make

this move and start over wavers. Shaking off my doubts, I unplug the air mattress from the wall. It would suck if I popped it by overfilling it. Then I grab my soup, relieved to see it has a pull open top so I don't have to hunt for my can opener. Can in hand, I stop, realizing I can't microwave it.

For some reason, partly since the tears were already so close to falling on their own, this is why I start crying. Sure, it's less about the bowl and spoon and more about missing my family but the tears fall all the same.

Grateful for my tissues, I blow my nose, sit on my air mattress, and have a good cry. About thirty or so minutes later I'm still hungry. Unpacking enough for soup and drug store wine, I eat. It may have been the most satisfying meal of my life.

Since Allen left me, I've had many meals. This one is different. It's a meal in a place that's all mine, a home he would never have approved of. In its current state, that is. He would hate everything about this place. Knowing that makes me love it even more.

My life was changing and this, right here, was the first step.

CHAPTER 2

Noah

"**M**ERRY CHRISTMAS," I mutter, dropping my bag in Gideon's lap.

I was surprised to see his truck in the parking lot of our family hardware store and figured I could save a trip to his place by giving them to him now.

"It's July," he argues, looking into the bag. Once he sees what's inside he squeezes the plastic bag shut with a groan. "You need to stop buying me condoms."

I shake my head, staring down at my younger brother with a grin. "Nope, this is my gift to the world."

"What's that?" Our dad asks as he walks in from the back.

"Nothing," Gideon grumbles, taking the bag and leaving.

Out of my three brothers, Gideon and I look the most alike. With light brown hair and blue eyes, there are times that looking at him feels like looking in a mirror. The biggest difference between us is the three inches I have on him, and the fact that I'm not trying to fuck every woman I see.

As soon as the door closes behind him, Dad turns to me. "What's gotten into him?"

"Noah bought him condoms again," Abby chirps, my ever-helpful little sister.

Dad coughs to cover his laugh. Gideon, my youngest brother is single-handedly trying to sleep his way through every single, and a couple not, woman in town.

"Someday some girl is going to turn his world upside down," Dad says under his breath.

Abby passes my dad a mug. "Want a bagel?"

He peeks into the bakery bag she brought. "Is the Pope catholic?" He jokes, and then asks, "You get any of those blueberry ones?"

Abby smirks at me before reaching into the bag for a blueberry bagel. They're his favorite and since Abby started stopping by the store every Monday morning with breakfast, she has always brought him one.

"You're a good girl." He smiles brightly at his only daughter when she passes it to him.

"Thanks Dad," she replies with a grin.

While people can tell we're siblings, Abby, along with my oldest brother, Eli, and younger brother, Asher, all have dad's dark brown hair, whereas Gideon and I favor our mother's coloring.

The store phone starts ringing and I frown when I see dad set down his bagel to answer it.

"Where's Eli?" I ask Abby.

She tilts her head toward our dad and motions for me to follow her.

"What's with all the secrecy?" I ask once we're in the paint aisle.

"He and Brooke are seeing a marriage counselor."

My brows lift. "Shit. Things that bad?"

"Don't say a word." She points a finger at me in warning. "Brooke and the kids moved in with her sister last week."

"Jesus. I can't believe Eli didn't tell me," I grumble angrily.

My little sister folds her arms across her chest and gives me a look. Eli and I can butt heads from time to time but I never thought he would keep something like this from me.

"Did he tell you?" I ask.

She shakes her head and for some reason that makes me feel better.

"Did he tell anyone?" I clarify.

She frowns. "Maybe Gideon since he said he was going to help Dad cover the store this morning, but that doesn't mean he told him where he was going."

"So does anyone know other than you?"

She turns to look toward the flat enamel paint cans. "You know how he is."

Can't argue that. Eli, our older brother, is a perfectionist and a giant pain in my ass. The last thing he'd want is for anyone to know he and Brooke were having marriage problems.

"How's he going to swing nobody noticing they're separated?"

With the whole family living so close, there's never a shortage of gatherings. Whether it's birthday parties, one of the kids' games or a random family dinner, we see each other plenty.

"Brooke has agreed to keep things under wraps as long as they're in counseling," she replies, her eyes returning to mine.

"Mom will flip if she finds out."

"Where'd you two go?" our dad calls out.

"Promise you won't say anything," Abby whispers.

I nod. "We're here old man."

Abby walks out of the aisle first and heads straight for my dad. She leans over the counter to press a kiss to his cheek and then gives me a wave. "I have to head to the office."

"See you later kiddo," Dad mutters.

She punches Gideon affectionately as she passes him on her way out the door. Since he no longer has the bag, I'm guessing he put them in his truck when he left.

After watching Abby walk out the door, Dad shifts his focus to me. "What are you still doing here?"

"You trying to get me out of here so you can eat my bagel?" I joke.

He fakes a grab at the bagel bag with a laugh.

"And you," he looks to Gideon, "you're never here this early."

Gideon shrugs, his light brown hair falling into his eyes. "Eli had a thing. Asked me to cover." He looks at me. "If I knew you'd be here I'd still be in bed."

I grab a bagel. "I'm just here for the food."

"Your boys working today?"

I nod my head. "They are. I'm meeting them over at the job site in a few. Abby texted me so I figured I'd stop by for a free breakfast."

"I thought you were getting free breakfast from that little bakery on Fifth," Gideon replies, throwing me under the bus.

"What's this?" Dad asks.

I glare at Gideon. "I was seeing the woman who owns that bakery. It's over now."

"Is Eli the only one who's going to give me grandchildren?" My dad grumbles.

Both Gideon and I groan.

"Well this was fun," I say, taking my bagel and moving toward the door.

"I was only giving you a hard time. I wasn't trying to run you off."

I wave him off. "It's cool. It's cool. I still gotta go."

"Are you coming to dinner Friday?" My dad calls after me.

"I'll be there," I reply, before pushing open the door.

I finish my bagel in my truck, my eyes on the entrance. Thompson Hardware has been in my family for three generations. This place is as much of a home to me as the house I grew up in.

I got my first tool belt before I started elementary school. It's no surprise I still wear one. In fact, growing up a Thompson rubbed off on all of us when it came to what careers we all chose.

Eli's running the store now since dad retired, I'm a building contractor, Asher's a carpenter, Abby's a realtor, and the baby, Gideon, is a landscape architect. I'm sure if one of us had wanted to help run the store Eli would have attempted to share control. Thankfully, since Eli would have failed miserably at that, our interests led us to carving out our own professions.

My team is working on the roof of a colonial style house not far from the store. A tree limb fell during a storm. Luckily, the homeowners were insured. After they finish the roof, my team is going to do some interior work to spots where there was water damage.

"Hey Noah," Jon calls from the front yard once I park.

Jon has been with me since the beginning. He manages the work sites and I handle the estimates and business side of the work, not that I don't have the skills to be right there with him at each job site. I'm just better than Jon is at the business side.

"How's it going?" I ask.

He looks toward the roof. "Shingles should be all up today. The water damage on the inside is worse than we thought. Mrs. Brown is home now. She'd like to talk to you about us replacing the subfloor and putting in new hardwoods on the second level."

"On it," I reply and head to the front door.

How she can hear my knocking over the shingles going in, I'm not sure.

"Hi Noah. How are you?"

"Good Mrs. Brown. Thank you. Hopefully the noise isn't too disruptive."

Her gaze shifts upward. "Better the noise than a hole in the roof."

I nod. "Jon mentioned you'd like to discuss us working on your floors."

She motions for me to follow her and I spend the next hour taking measurements as she points out the places the water damaged the floor. I write up a quote based on the labor and basic materials with a second quote for the higher end wood flooring she wanted. She'll need to have the additional damage inspected by her insurance guy. She's a good customer and will not only pay her invoices on time, but she'll also tell all of her friends if we do a good job. Since we do kickass work, she'll definitely tell her friends.

After meeting with Mrs. Brown, I head back to the

front yard to Jon. "We'll have to wait to hear if her insurance company will approve the work. Even if they don't, I think she'll still do the floors since insurance covered the cost of the roof."

Jon nods. "Sounds good. What's the schedule look like for next week?"

I have an electronic planner app on my phone that syncs with his. Problem is, he never looks at it. Knowing that, I also print off a hardcopy showing the next two weeks of work and give it to him every Monday.

We all have our strengths and weaknesses, Jon and I have a great partnership because we balance each other out.

"I'm off to the Johnson's to take some measurements. They want a quote on a three-season screened-in porch."

"If we finish the roof today, we're going to start on the ceiling damage. I'll text you to let you know far along we get before we quit for the day."

I lift my chin in farewell and walk to my truck. The Johnson's place is clear on the other side of Woodlake. It's a decent drive, one long enough to give me time to think.

The news that Eli is having marriage problems is not good. Their kids, Ethan, Aiden, and Connie are dealing with this crap and I don't even know if they have talked to anyone about it.

His wife, Brooke, is nice enough. Other than knowing her through Eli and exchanging small talk with her at family events, I'm not tight with her. She's a good mom, and a cool person. Hell, she's had to be a saint to put up with Eli's shit.

What I don't know is, how kindly she'd take to me calling her out of the blue to check on their kids. Eli's a pain in the ass for not telling us what's going on and I'm a shit brother for not noticing, and an even shittier uncle for not being there for my niece and nephews.

Thing is, Eli is the only one of us who's proved settling down and staying that way is possible. I date, but none of the women interest me long term. All Gideon does is dick around, Asher's turning into a fucking hermit and Abby doesn't date at all.

After this appointment, I'll call Abby. She's the only one who seems to know what's going on.

I rush through my meeting with Mrs. Johnson. I was expecting her husband to be there, but his presence may have interrupted her attempts to put her hand in my pants. I might not have many rules when it comes to the women I see, but not being married is one of them.

If she goes with our estimate, I'll need to discuss with Jon if it will be worth it to take the job. I can steer clear of the worksite but I'm not sure it would matter. It's possible she could harass Jon or our crew while they work. That could cause delays, not to mention the potential concerns of an irate husband if he found out what his wife was up to.

Not wanting to call Abby from Mrs. Johnson's house, I wait until I'm at a restaurant nearby to do it.

She's normally with clients whenever I call, so when she answers, I'm pleasantly surprised.

"Hey Noah, what's up?"

"I was thinking about what you said this morning and wanted to talk about it."

"I figured," she murmurs. "Where are you?"

"Winston's."

"Have you ordered yet?" She asks, and then adds, "I'm not far. I can meet you for lunch."

"I'm still sitting in my truck."

"Go get us a table. I'll be there in five," she orders.

I smile at her words. I'm seven years older, I'm close to a foot taller than her, and weigh at least fifty pounds more than she does, but she bosses me around like a champ. I'm seated by the time she shows. She reaches out, giving my shoulder a squeeze before sliding into the booth across from me.

"Have they taken drink orders yet?"

Her greeting is rushed in a way that makes me pause. When I saw her this morning she seemed fine. Now, there's tension blanketing her usual sunny mood.

I shake my head. "Everything okay?"

She starts digging in her giant purse and pulls out a file. "I need to stop by a house I sold to pick up my lockbox. I was wondering if you wanted to come with me. The place is a heap and the woman who bought it is in way over her head. She's planning to do all the work herself. Maybe you can talk some sense into her."

She slides the folder across the table to me. I open it to see she wasn't exaggerating when she said the house was a heap.

"Has it been condemned?" I ask, looking at the pictures.

Abby cringes, shaking her head then her face brightens and she says, "She did have the place rewired before she moved in."

I let out a breath. "Thank God for that. Does the furnace work?"

"An inspection was done. It works, but barely. I doubt it will make it through the winter," she winces.

"She isn't planning on living there during the remodel, is she?" I ask.

Her face falls and her mouth stays clamped shut. My

little sister has never been known to hold her tongue.

"At least tell me this isn't her first remodel," I push.

Her gaze skitters away.

"Abby," I warn and her eyes move back to me.

Her hands come up, to punctuate as she explains, "I've only ever talked to her over the phone. From what I know, she made a killing off the place she sold in Texas. I don't know what's bringing her out here but it didn't sound like she's lived anywhere else.

What I do know is, she bought it outright, no financing, and she had an inspection done. The place was sold as is, but the inspector said the foundation looked good. Other than that, it's in crap shape. So she's out here, possibly all alone and could maybe use a good contractor."

I blink at her then I look back at the file, memorizing the address. Yes, I'm a business man, but that doesn't mean I'm heartless.

I flip the folder shut and slide it back to her. "I can't look at it anymore if I don't want to lose my appetite. When are you going over?"

"Ha-ha," she grumbles, taking it and pushing it back into her purse. "I planned on heading there from here."

"I have an appointment. I might be able to swing by later today or tomorrow. Or, since you're going you can just give her one of my cards."

"You should go by and meet her. If she decides to hire someone it'll help if you've already had a conversation and seen the place in person."

Our server comes and takes our drink and food orders.

Once she's gone, Abby changes the subject and asks, "What'd you want to talk about?"

"How serious do you think this separation is?"

She drums her fingers on the tabletop. "It can't be good if the kids and her are at her mom's."

"I get that I'm not supposed to know about this, but we have to do something."

She nods. "I feel the same way, but I'm at a loss as to what to do."

Our drinks come and I toy with the paper wrapper of my straw. "How tight are you with Brooke?"

She takes a sip of her soda. "I like her. I think we're cool but it's not like we share secrets. I could try and call her, but it'd piss off Eli and I have no idea what I'd even say to her."

"Did Eli tell you what her reason was for leaving him?" I ask.

She nods then frowns. "I know what he said, but if that's the whole story I'm not sure. He told me she felt like they were drifting apart, that he worked too much and she was sick of feeling like a single parent."

As much as it sucks to admit it, those aren't unreasonable grievances. He's bossy to a fault and a perfectionist. When he took over the store, it was like an obsession for him to prove he could not only keep it running but make it more profitable to prove he was doing a good job.

"Fucking Eli," I mutter.

She doesn't argue.

"At least he agreed to the counseling. He's a pain in the ass, but if he didn't want to work things out with Brooke, he never would have done that."

She nods. "Does that mean we should wait and see?"

"We could try and reach out to Brooke to check on the kids," I suggest.

Our food comes. I dive in but Abby only lifts her fork and stares down at her plate.

"I was planning to do that anyway, maybe offer to take them for a night to give her a break," she says quietly.

Between bites of my burger and fries, I reply, "You should do that. Try and get a read on her. If she's cool with you taking the kids, that has to mean she isn't planning to completely write off the rest of the family even if she's pissed with Eli."

She nods. "I can do that. If you want, as soon as we're done eating I'll call her from the parking lot."

I offer her my fist across the table and she presses hers to mine.

We finish eating, switching our topics to something lighter. I pay then we head outside, and I wait while she calls.

"Hey Brooke, it's Abby," she greets, her eyes on mine.

She pauses as Brooke says something.

Then she says, "I talked to Eli and, well, I know you guys are going through a rough patch."

There's another pause, this one Abby nods through.

"I don't want to get in between you guys but I did want to offer my help with the kids if you needed it and, not only if you need it but because I want to. I love those kids and thought they might like to go see a movie with their aunt Abby."

She reaches for my arm and squeezes it.

"What?" I mouth.

She lets go of my arm and lifts her finger in a hold on gesture.

Then she presses her hand to her chest and closes her eyes in what looks like relief. "Thank you. Yes. I completely understand. I know how my brother is. I'll check movie times and call you back. Okay, Okay. Bye."

Abby hangs up and drops her phone into her purse. "She said yes."

"I gathered," I reply. "Call me after the movie to tell me how it went."

She nods. "Where are you off to now?"

I smirk. "I have an appointment. Depending on how long it goes I might be able to swing by that house you showed me. I have a feeling the woman who bought it is going to need a contractor. If you can wait till later this afternoon we can go together."

She smiles but shakes her head. "I need to go now. My afternoon is booked but I knew if I showed you that file you wouldn't be able to resist."

"Brat," I grumble, pulling her into a headlock so I can mess up her hair.

"Get off you big jerk," she shouts, trying to step on my foot.

I kiss the top of her head and let her go. She mutters under her breath that she wished she had sisters as she smooths down her hair.

CHAPTER 3

Finley

I T TOOK LONGER than it should have, but I got my trailer unloaded. When I sold the house in Texas, I also downsized my belongings. Whatever reminded me of Allen, or didn't make me happy, I sold, donated, or trashed. Even knowing I'd have to replace some of what I got rid of, I still did it.

Letting go of so much made unpacking what was left all that much easier. It still sucked, but it could have been so much worse. After I emptied the trailer, I turned it into the U-Haul drop off. The guy working the counter made a point of using hand sanitizer once he was done with me. Considering I didn't even cough or sneeze on him, it seemed excessive on his part.

After a quick grocery run, I'm surprised to see a woman knocking on my kitchen door when I pull up. Her head turns at the sound of my squeaky brakes.

She looks like she's about my age, or maybe a couple of years younger, and even from the distance between my car and the kitchen door, I can tell she's gorgeous. In heels and a fancy business suit, she sticks out like a sore thumb next to my fixer upper. I resist the urge to flip the visor and look in the mirror before getting out of the car. I'm certain I look like hell and don't need to confirm it.

"Ms. Reeves?" She asks as soon as I open my car door, walking toward me.

Hurriedly, I slide out of my seat and get out of the car. "Yes, that's me. Can I help you?"

She waits until I have the car door shut to offer me her hand. "I'm Abby Thompson, the realtor. I thought I'd swing by to see if you got in okay and to pick up my lockbox."

Pulling my hand back, I warn, "I'm sick, way sick, the plague. You may not want to shake my hand."

Her hand doesn't waver. "Germs don't scare me."

Deciding I like her, I slip my hand into hers and give it a shake. "It's so nice to finally meet you."

"You as well." She looks past me and must see the grocery bags on my backseat. "Need a hand bringing those in?"

"Oh, you don't have to . . ."

She cuts me off with a wave of her hand. "I'm happy to."

With her help, and the fact that I didn't get that much, it takes only one trip.

"Thank you," I say, setting my bags down on the floor.

Her eyes move around the space and I hope it doesn't smell as badly as it did before. "I have to admit. I didn't believe you when you said you were going to live here during the reno."

"It's not so bad," I lie.

There's pure hope in her tone when she asks. "Have you done this before?"

I shake my head, and then wish I hadn't. My sinuses are still killing me.

With wide eyes she asks, "Will you have any help?"

"Does the internet count?" I joke.

She doesn't laugh. "Please promise you'll call me if it ends up being more than you can handle on your own."

"I'll be fine," I say, only half believing myself.

She nods and glances at her watch. "I need to run, but if it's alright with you I'd like to swing by again another day. You're new to not only Woodlake, but also New Hampshire. I meant to put together a little welcome kit but ran out of time."

"You don't have to, " I reply, not wanting to take up more of her time.

"I'm happy to. I already started it by grabbing menus from the best restaurants around here. That alone will save you time learning the places to avoid."

My budget doesn't have much room in it for takeout. Still, I reply, "Thank you. That sounds great."

Her eyes sweep my space again. "I'll let myself out."

I follow her the few steps to the kitchen door. "You need to give it a good tug."

She does, opening it on one pull.

After she leaves, I call the local waste pickup company to schedule the delivery of a dumpster. Once that's done, I scrub the half bath on the main level.

There are two full bathrooms upstairs but they both need to be gutted to fix whatever made the plumbing fail. For now, the water is turned off to both. Until they're fixed, I'll be washing my hair and bathing the best I can from the downstairs bathroom sink.

Would Allen turn up his nose in disgust at the idea of me washing up from a sink in a small bathroom with ugly fixtures and wallpaper? Absolutely.

That fact alone has me charmed by the idea.

Screw him.

Stage one of my remodel is to gut the kitchen and den. I plan to work and sleep in the front rooms while I start working on the back.

I can see it finished in my head. More than that, I can see myself in this house once it's done. Outside there's snow through the window, making everything look like a dreamy winter wonderland while I'm snuggled up on a plush sofa, a throw blanket across my lap and a glass of wine in my hand as I gaze serenely into a glowing fire.

The vision is so clear in my mind, it's what has kept me moving forward despite the concerns of my family and my own doubts. I'm not under any delusions that this is going to be quick or easy.

"You can do this," I mutter to myself, collapsing onto my air mattress.

I've done everything I can today. It would be pointless to start gutting the kitchen before the dumpster is delivered. Plus, maybe some sleep will help the sinus pressure in my head go away.

God, it's more like a pounding. No, wait, there's actual pounding.

I lift my head and look toward the front door. I can't see it from where I'm laying but that doesn't stop me from trying. Could the dumpster people be here already?

I shift up onto my elbow. The guy on the phone made it sound like it would be tomorrow at the earliest. I groan when I hear another knock at the door.

Getting to my feet, I power my way to the door. When I open it, I squint at the man on the other side.

"What are you doing here?" I ask, before sneezing on

him.

The floor I'm standing on is somewhat rotted. If I'm lucky, maybe it will crack, splinter, and swallow me whole.

He grins at me before lifting the hem of his shirt to wipe my snot from his face. I sneezed all over the hot guy buying condoms at the convenience store.

"Bless you," he chuckles.

"I'm so sorry." I gesture toward his face.

He shakes his head, fighting a smile. "It's okay."

Okay?

Nothing about this is okay. How is he standing right in front of me? My eyes take him in, from his faded cargo shorts to his fitted navy blue t-shirt, the shade accentuating his ocean blue eyes. Pushing past my mortification I ask, "Is there something I can help you with?"

He offers me his hand, "I'm Noah Thompson. Abby is my sister."

Condom guy is my realtor's brother?

Wondering if he recognizes me, I slip my hand into his. "Hi. I'm Finley Wiltshire, I mean Reeves."

He tilts his head to the side. "Which one is it, Wiltshire or Reeves?"

I don't know why I even said Wiltshire.

"Reeves," I reply, folding my arms over my chest. "Now, why is the brother of my realtor knocking on my door?"

"She didn't tell you I'd be stopping by?"

When I shake my head he goes on. "She showed me pictures of," he makes a point of looking right, up, left, and then back to me before saying, "your house and told me you plan to remodel it on your own."

"And?" I press.

His right eyebrow moves up a fraction. "I'm a contractor. I could tell this was a big project just by the pictures. Now seeing the place in person I know it's worse."

"And?" I repeat, not liking where this is going.

"This project is too big for one person to tackle alone," he replies.

My brows knit. "Says who?"

His head jerks. "Me. I just said it."

"You don't know that," I argue.

He lifts his hand and rubs his face before asking. "You lift?"

"What?" I ask.

He shrugs. "Do you lift weights?"

"No-no," I stammer, wondering why he would ask.

Is he implying that I'm not strong enough to do this? My heart starts pounding. I spent years being told I was inadequate; I'm done with that bullshit.

"I'm tougher than I look," I blurt.

My words sound strong, until I sniffle.

Noah presses his lips together. "I have no doubt."

"There are tools I can rent to lift the things I can't lift on my own."

"Fair point," he nods his head in agreement. "But, if you can't lift it, how are you going to get it onto the tool?"

I frown, why hadn't I thought of that? "Fine. Well I can hire help for those parts."

"Do you have any experience with construction?"

I shake my head, the movement aggravating the

pressure behind my eyes. I press my fingers to my temple.

"Hey, are you okay?" He asks, resting his hand on my arm.

I shake off his touch. "It's only a bad head cold."

"You look like you should lie down," he suggests in a tone that says no arguing.

I ignore his tone and start to protest anyway. His hand moves back to my arm and he turns me, his other arm coming to rest on the small of my back as he guides me back into my own house.

"You don't have to," I groan.

My words do nothing to stop him.

"Of course," he grunts when he sees my air mattress.

For a second I care, for a second I even consider what my current situation would look like from the outside. Then I remember this man is no one to me, why should I give a rat's ass about his opinion.

"You can leave now," I snap.

"You lie down. I'm going to take some measurements."

He'll do what?

"You will absolutely not. I don't care whose brother you are. You will leave right now or I'm calling the police," I warn.

He tilts his head to the side. "You'd actually kick out free help?"

Wait. Free?

I cross my arms over my chest and squint at him. "Why would you do that?"

He shrugs and it's annoying how attractive he looks doing it. "Consider it my good deed for the year."

"That's crazy. You don't even know me," I press.

He inhales, and I watch his chest fill with it. "I don't like the idea of you trying to do this all on your own."

"You can't just come into my house and order me around." I snap.

"I wasn't planning on it." He counters.

I scrunch up my face.

He smiles and suddenly I feel out of breath.

"I think I need to sit down," I mumble, turning back toward my air mattress.

His smile falls and he follows me. "Are you sure you're okay? There's an urgent care not far from here I can take you to if you want."

I gesture behind me. "No, I'm fine. A good night of sleep is all I need."

I hear movement behind me but I keep my eyes forward. God, this cold is kicking my ass.

I sit on the mattress and moments later Noah is pressing a bottle of water into my hand.

"Fluids will help," he says.

I somehow manage not to laugh at the fact that he sounds like my mother. He walks back toward my kitchen. I take a drink and look around for my tissues. I should have bought more, and then I could have scattered them all around.

"Is there a box of tissues in there?" I call.

There's a chuckle, followed by footsteps as he returns, box of tissues in hand. "Here you go."

As soon as I'm done blowing my nose, he asks, "What are your plans for this place?"

My brows pull together in confusion. "What do you mean?"

He gestures to the space around us. "Are you planning to work with the bones of the space as it stands now or do you plan to take down existing walls and put up new ones?"

"Oh," I reply, understanding dawning. "I'm leaving the walls where they are. I spoke to someone in the permits office and I don't need to file permits for the stuff I'm doing. The electrician had to have his work inspected though. That was done a couple of weeks ago."

"Who did you use?" He asks, his eyes moving to a spot in the wall where the new wiring is exposed.

I squeeze my eyes shut as I try to remember his name. "I think there was a D in his name." I open my eyes and see he's grinning at me. "Your sister gave me his name."

"Damon Breyer?"

I nod. "Yes, that's the man who did it."

"That's good. Work wise, what did you plan on tackling first?"

I lie back on the mattress and stare up at the ceiling. "First I'm going to tear out all the bad stuff." There's a chuckle at my use of stuff but I ignore it and keep talking. "Then I was going to put new not bad stuff in."

I blink when his face comes into view as he leans over my air mattress. "That makes sense but I'm going to need some specifics when it comes to flooring soon."

I shift up to a seated position and he backs away. "I was planning on going slow because of my budget."

"What is your budget?"

When I give him the figure he blinks before saying, "It's a good thing your new partner gets a discount on materials."

I press my fingers to my temples. "Why would you do all this?"

35

"You're acting like it's a bad thing." His smile leaves me winded again.

I pull in a breath. "This is a lot to take in."

"All I want is to help you fix this place up so you won't have to sleep on an air mattress in your living room."

I want to ask why but don't. "I'm sorry. You're being so nice and your offer is incredibly generous. I just moved here and, is this what people from New Hampshire are like?"

His mouth twitches and he ignores my question to ask one of his own. "What's your number?"

I tilt my head to the side. "You want my number?"

He pulls a phone from his back pocket. "Yep."

Yesterday I saw him buying condoms. Could this all be some elaborate ruse to get in my pants?

"I'm not going to sleep with you," I blurt.

His eyes narrow. It's not fair that he looks even hotter when he's annoyed.

"I saw all those condoms you bought. Maybe this is your come on strategy."

"My come on strategy?" He repeats, his head turned slightly to the left.

I nod.

"Let me get this right," he starts. "I seek out women with colds, who recently bought houses that should have been condemned and donate my time and energy helping them as a ploy to seduce them?"

"Well when you put it like that." I bite my lip and look away, hoping he assumes the blush on my cheeks is just from my cold.

He laughs, and then asks for my number again.

This time I give it to him.

"Think of it as your lucky day," he says.

"My lucky day," I repeat, my brows coming together.

"Exactly," he replies.

Shaking my head, I argue. "This is too insane. You know nothing about me. I could be a horrible person that you'd wish you never met."

"If you were, you wouldn't be trying to talk me out of helping you."

Okay, he has a point there.

"How about this, you sleep on it, and I'll call you tomorrow?"

"Why do I have a feeling if I say no tomorrow you'll just figure out another way to talk me into it?" I ask.

He shrugs, and then looks around my space again. "Maybe I consider this my civic duty."

"Why? What's in it for you?"

"A couple of things. One, I love fixing up houses and it's been a while since I've worked on one in this condition, and two, my own peace of mind that you don't freeze to death or have the roof collapse on you."

"The inspector said the roof was in okay shape," I argue even though most of what he said was nice.

"Did he mention the stage after okay is shit?"

I can't help it, I laugh. This entire situation is ridiculous. I'm insane to be fighting help but I'm still a single woman in a new place and I can't be too careful.

"Have you thought about replacing your furnace?" He asks, ignoring my laugh.

I sober. "I hoped I wouldn't need to do that until next year."

"How about you think about letting me help tonight, but you give me your answer tomorrow when I come back with a buddy to look at your furnace? He'll be able to say for sure if it'll make it through the winter."

"There's a wood stove in the den," I add.

"Has it been inspected, and do you know the last time it was cleaned?" He shoots back.

Frowning, I shake my head. "I don't know. It wasn't listed in the inspection report."

He looks up at the ceiling before his gaze comes back to me and he orders, "You have to ask for them to look at it. If it wasn't in your report it wasn't done. No fires in any of the fireplaces or the stove until I've looked at them."

He sounds so serious, all I can do is nod.

His voice lowers as his face softens. "You don't know me and I get that I'm coming off pushy. I'm sorry but that's just who I am. I'm not trying to be a dick, but there are legitimate safety issues with fixing up an old house like this. I do this for a living and I'm damn good at it. You want the lead on this, take it. You tell me what you want to do and I'll show you how to do it safely and the right way so you're not having to pay someone else to fix it later."

"You'll let me be in charge?" I ask, my tone uncertain.

He nods. After ten years of having no control, him nodding feels like a victory.

Pushing up off of my air mattress, I cross the room and hold out my hand to him. "I don't have to think about it. I accept your offer."

His large hand grips mine, warmth from his palm melting into my skin. "Then it's a deal."

I move to pull my hand back but he holds it a beat longer. My eyes lock on his and he lets go.

I take a couple steps back. "I think the dumpster is

being delivered tomorrow, in case the drive is blocked off when you get here."

"Good call on ordering one." His eyes never leaving mine.

I blush, which has to be a random heat flash from my cold and not a reaction to his words because that would be crazy. No, this whole thing, our deal, is already crazy; blushing because he complimented me would be insane.

"Seemed like the sensible thing to do."

He nods. "It was a pleasure meeting you Finley."

I follow him back to the front door.

He pauses on my doorstep and looks at the tangled mess of weeds and bushes clogging up the walkway.

I grab his elbow and tug. "You should go out the kitchen door."

His gaze moves to my hand and I drop it as if burned. "Do you want to save any of this?"

Shaking my head, I grasp my hands together behind my back.

"I'll bring something to spray it down with when I come tomorrow. My brother is a landscaper. This stuff will kill what's growing and make clearing it a breeze."

"That sounds great," I reply, grateful since I had planned to prune and pull it all by hand.

He eyes travel over my face before. "Go get some sleep. You need your rest."

"Thank you for all of this."

That makes him grin for some reason. "Don't thank me yet. I haven't done anything."

"Okay," I reply making his grin shift into a smile.

"See you tomorrow Finley."

He turns to leave.

"Fin," I correct.

He pauses on the step and looks back at me.

"My friends call me Fin," I say.

"Go get some rest Fin," he replies making me smile.

I watch him make his way down my overgrown walk and then get into his truck before I close and lock the door.

After that conversation, I pull the cheap bottle of white wine from the fridge and pour myself a large glass. Then I make my way back to my air mattress, wine finished by the time I reach it. As I settle down onto it, and get the pillow under my head just right, I wonder what I've gotten myself into before I pass out.

CHAPTER 4

Noah

I WANT HER. It's been years since I've been this attracted to a woman. Everything about her, from her back off stance, searching hazel eyes, full pouty lips, and gentle curves calls to me.

She sneezed on me.

I laugh out loud and then shake my head.

What the hell have I gotten myself into? Today did not go as planned. I walked up to that house hoping to generate a little business. Within a minute of talking to Finley I knew I'd agree to just about anything, helping her fix up that God damned house, to spend more time with her.

Helping her covers two bases. I get to be close to her, and keep her from injuring herself. I must be losing my mind.

If my brothers find out I'm crazy for a woman I've just met, they'll never let me live it down. When I get to my office, I call Abby.

"How'd it go?" she asks instead of saying hello.

"You should have talked her out of buying it," I grumble.

But if she had, I never would have met her.

"I was the agent for the seller. She came to me," she argues.

I lean back in my chair and prop my feet up onto my desk. "It's a mess Abby."

"Are you going to help her?"

My eyes shift to the mountain of paperwork on my desk. "Yeah."

There's silence on the line before she pushes further, "What aren't you telling me?"

Abby has an uncanny ability to hear things unsaid.

"I'm going to help her," I reply defensively.

"So she hired you?" She says.

"Not exactly."

"Noah," she warns.

I laugh at her tone. She inherited it from our mom.

"I'm going to help her as a friend," I explain.

"As a friend," she scoffs. "You've known her a day."

"That's true," I say.

There's noise in the background. "I have to go, my client just got here. As soon as I'm done, I'm calling you back and you're going to tell me everything."

"Alright Abs. Talk to you later."

My next call would be to Gideon, but since he never answers his phone I send him a text instead. He surprises me by calling me.

"Hey," I answer.

"What do you need my destroyer spray for?" He asks by way of answering.

"Don't worry about it," I reply nonchalantly, hoping not to pique his interest.

"Fine," he grumbles before hanging up on me.

I stare at my phone and shake my head. Then I set it on my desk and get to work. Last thing I need to think about right now is Gideon sniffing around her. There's a reason I buy him condoms in bulk. I'd hate to have to kick his ass for even looking at Finley.

Two hours later the pile is significantly smaller.

"Knock, knock."

At the sound of my sister's voice, I look up to see Abby peeking into my office.

"I thought you were going to call." I move, shifting to my feet.

She pushes the door open and crosses the room to me. "I can't tell when you're hiding stuff over the phone."

I hug her. "What could I possibly have to hide?"

Letting her go, I move back to my desk and motion for her to sit in one of the armchairs that face it.

"Don't try and BS me. What's the deal with you and Finley?"

I deflect. "How well do you know her?"

"Ahh, pumping me for information about her. That must mean you're interested in more than just her house."

I shrug, neither confirming nor denying her words.

She leans back in her chair before toeing off her heels and crossing one leg over the other. "She got the house for a steal, even considering its condition. She paid for it outright and while I was obviously not the realtor on the sale of her house in Texas, I do know she made decent money on it and used that to pay for the rewiring. She plans to use more of it to start the remodel.

"She's going to work from home. She does some kind of remote customer service thing for a travel insurance company."

She pauses, waiting for me to respond. As a contractor, what she told me should be everything I would normally care about. In this case, with Fin, it's not.

"Do you know anything about her personally?" I ask, and by asking make it clear my interest is more than professional.

Abby starts the smile, but catches herself from grinning outright. "She's recently divorced."

That explains the two last names she gave me.

"If she has children, which I don't think she does, they're staying in Texas. She's sweet and easy to work with. In any real estate transaction there are a ton of forms to sign. She was prompt and didn't complain about the process. She was also understanding with the owners. I like her."

Finley's hazel eyes flash in my mind and I admit, "I like her too."

This time she does grin.

"Was that your plan in sending me over there?" I ask.

Abby has a bit of a matchmaker in her. If this was her ploy, it wouldn't be her first attempt at it.

"There was something about her that reminded me of you," she replies.

"Care to share what it was?" I ask when she doesn't elaborate.

"She's a grounded dreamer," she explains.

I blink.

What the hell does that mean?

When I don't say anything, she goes on. "Eli is all

grounded, no room for exceptions, total stickler for the rules and stubborn as hell. Asher is in his own dream world, and we're lucky he remembers we exist, and Gideon is used to getting whatever he wants whenever he wants it."

Her descriptions of our brothers are pretty spot on. "And I'm a grounded dreamer?"

She nods, pleased with herself. "Yep, you've got a bit of all of them since you're older, Asher and Gideon got those traits from you."

"Don't let Gideon hear you say that," I joke.

She shakes her head. "He gets defensive when you give him advice. He thinks you try to parent him."

The remark hits home because it drives me crazy when Eli bosses me around. "Do you think I try to parent him?"

She grimaces. "You have your moments."

"But dreamer?" I lift my hands to show off my office. "It's not like my head is in the clouds. Running a contracting company is about as grounded as it gets."

She shifts in her chair. "You're taking me too literally. You're grounded in your work and a dreamer in the rest of your life. You've dated, a couple of times seriously but never asked a woman to live with you and broke up with the ones that asked you to move in with them. You're thirty-eight years old and a great guy. You haven't been able to settle down because you're a—"

"Dreamer," I mutter, cutting her off. "I lived with someone after college."

She cocks her head to the side, her jaw going slack. "Who?"

I shake my head, happy to still have one part of my life a secret.

She frowns and I suspect the minute she leaves my office she'll call our mom to pump her for info. Annoying her has never stopped being fun.

"Are you going to ask her out?" She finally asks.

I shrug. "Maybe."

"Don't boss her around," Abby warns.

"Grounded dreamer," I murmur, then I add, "I promise I'll go easy on her."

She stands, slipping her shoes back on one by one. "I want updates."

"I love you too," I tease.

She pauses in the doorway of my office. "Updates."

I shake my head as I watch her leave.

"Noah, it's almost four," my assistant Justin calls from the hallway.

"Shit," I grumble.

I lost track of time when Abby stopped by. Now if I don't move my ass, I'm going to be late for a client consult.

"I'm leaving. If they call, tell them I'm on my way."

He nods.

When I hit the main door, I look back at him. "The files on the left are ready for invoices."

Justin lifts his chin in ascent. He's one of Jon's sons. We took him on a couple years ago to help around the office. He handles the phone messages and keeps me from double booking Jon or myself.

He's still in college. Jon is paying his tuition and he still lives at home so he's working for spending cash. Once his classes are done, he comes in after lunch and works until five, sometimes six.

He's a good kid. Jon wishes he'd go into contracting,

but his current major is chemical engineering. Jon blames his wife Emily. She's a middle school science teacher.

With moderate disregard for speed limits, I make it to my four o'clock appointment on time. The meeting doesn't go as well as I had hoped. They already had a competing bid that ended up being a lot less than our quote. I couldn't tell them the company they were choosing, Hill Top, did shit work and cut corners.

"If you change your mind. You know where to reach me," I reply, offering the client my hand.

I call Jon from their driveway to give him the bad news. They're wrapping up at the job site so he asks if I want to meet him for a drink. There's a bar near the office that we decide to meet at.

I get there first and order a draft for both of us. Jon shows not long after, slides onto the stool next to mine and takes a long pull from his drink.

Jon gives me a half smile. "Tell me about this woman."

I blink. "How'd you find out?"

He grins. "Em bumped into Abby."

Fucking gossipy little sisters.

I scratch the back of my head. "She's cute."

"Cute usually isn't what you go for," Jon replies.

He's right. I'm no monk, no strings was what normally turned me on before Fin.

"She sneezed on me," I laugh.

He nods his head, seeming to understand that odd statement.

I shake my head, hoping to get some understanding myself. "I can't explain it."

"Em slipped and fell." He smiles and lifts his

shoulders.

"What?"

He spins his stool to face me. "The first time I saw her, Emily slipped and fell. There were a bunch of us out skating on some pond and she was in front of me on the ice. I noticed her legs and was working up the nerve to try and talk to her when she fell on her ass. She laughed at herself, tried to get back on her feet and then fell again. I stopped to help her up and the rest is history, so I get you."

"Don't get ahead of yourself," I caution.

"Emily will want to meet her," he replies, twisting his stool back to face forward.

"Should I expect a call?" I ask.

His wife is as nosy as Abby is. He smiles, which confirms my suspicion.

"I'm going to tell her about the sneeze. She'll love that shit."

It's pointless to tell him not to. Jon and Emily tell each other everything. I'm going to regret sharing that.

I drink my beer. For the first time, it hits me that when we leave this bar, Jon's going home to his wife and family and I'm going home to my empty house.

"Want another?" I ask when he finishes his drink.

He shakes his head. "I'll buy you one if you're staying but I need to go. I'm in charge of getting Brit to her piano lesson since Emily is taking Joey to a Scout meeting."

"How do you remember all of this but you need weekly schedule printouts?" I joke.

It isn't a new joke.

He taps his head and chuckles. "Only got room for so much. You staying for another?"

I nod. He signals the bartender and leaves enough bills on the bar top to cover another beer.

"Thanks man."

He pats my back. "See you later."

"Tell Emily and the kids I said hi."

He pauses. "Still on for Thursday?"

"I'll be there," I reply.

He leaves and I pick up the food menu. I end up having dinner at this bar more nights than I'd like to admit.

"Mind if I join you?" A female asks from beside me.

Turning my head, I see an attractive tall blonde standing behind the stool Jon was sitting in.

"I'm not much company," I reply, my eyes moving back to the menu.

"Let me be the judge of that," she says, sliding onto the stool.

I push the menu away; I've memorized it ages ago.

Her hand moves in front of me. "I'm Angie."

I shake her hand. "Noah."

She grins. "I wouldn't say no to riding your ark."

Yep, she's so clever. I've never heard that joke or some version of it.

I'm saved from having to respond by the bartender coming over to take Angie's drink order. Instead of ordering food, like I had intended, I use this opportunity to finish my second beer and slip away.

Angie seemed nice enough but I wasn't interested, in small talk or whatever else she was hoping for. All I wanted was to eat in peace. I get takeout and have all the peace I can get eating in my living room in front of the TV.

I have a simple two-bedroom ranch style house. The

attached two-car garage is what made me buy it. Jon and I didn't have a separate office back then so I used half of it to store our tools and office files. We decided to rent the office space when our business grew. It helps to have a place where we can meet with clients and their designers. My garage worked for storage but not for much more.

Even after we started working out of the office, I stayed living here instead of moving to a bigger place. What's the point? I have a guest bedroom and all the space I need for myself.

Abby claims it needs a woman's touch. She tried giving me multicolored pillows to put on the sofa but I ended up throwing them into the spare bedroom. Then she tried to hang up pictures of trees. After I threatened to take away her spare key, she stopped. I don't have anything against trees, or artwork in general. The prints currently hanging in my place are old but ones I picked out myself. When it's time to change them, I pick out what replaces them, not my kid sister.

For having remodeled my kitchen myself, it doesn't get much use. The cabinets are dark walnut with custom under cabinet lighting. All that work and the thing I use most in it is the fridge. I open it now to grab a fresh beer.

When I'm done with my food, I shove the cardboard containers onto the rest of the cardboard containers already filling my trashcan. It's a reminder of how often I eat alone. I'm not lonely. I'm too busy with work, friends, and my family.

This Thursday I'm having dinner over at Jon's place. This weekend, I have a dinner at my folks with the rest of the family. We'll see if Brooke shows with the kids, and if she doesn't what excuse Eli will give for their absence.

I'm not sure what has me thinking about my

somewhat singular existence. I never noticed the takeout containers filling my trash or the fact that I'd be coming home to an empty house before today.

Something about seeing Finley in that big house all by herself triggered something. I didn't like knowing that she was alone. Even from our first meeting in that drug store, she captured my attention in a way the blonde at the bar never could.

I have an almost visceral need to take care of her. Knowing she's sick, alone, and camped out on a crappy air mattress is driving me nuts.

She has no one to watch over her. It wouldn't be good to go back over there tonight. She needs her rest. I can wait until I see her tomorrow. Yeah, I told her I'd call first but I've changed my mind since then.

My schedule is open tomorrow morning. I'll go over early. With that decided, I settle as well.

My bedroom is my favorite room in my house. It's the one spot in my house that a guest needs to be invited into. It's also where I display my favorite things. There's no rhyme or reason to them; there's a framed picture Aiden drew, the hockey puck from my first varsity game, and a pair of vintage skis I mounted over my bed. I also got a good king-sized mattress and a matching set to go with it. The furniture is solid mahogany and well made.

As I relax against my pillows I wonder what all of Finley's dark brown hair would look like spread across them.

CHAPTER 5

Finley

WHO ON EARTH is making all that noise? I'm still getting used to the sounds of the new place. This street, and the fact that I'm the last house on it, makes it much quieter than my old house. It's not that Woodlake is a smaller city than Springfield, in fact, population wise it's bigger.

It took some tossing and turning before I fell asleep but once I did, I slept like the dead last night. I'm only assuming it's morning because of the bright rays dancing across the wall, but I have no idea what time it is. What I do know is I could have slept another hour or two if it wasn't for all that racket going on outside.

Stubbornly, I turn onto my side, pulling my blanket over my face as I try to block out the noise. It doesn't work, if anything, it gets louder.

I crawl off the air mattress and slowly stand. I slept hard but, as my aching muscles protest, not comfortably. One thing that is better than yesterday is my head cold.

I can breathe through my nose. I inhale to confirm

and not only can I breathe, but I can do it through both nostrils.

My sinus pressure is nowhere near as bad as it was either. My throat, on the other hand, is not great. Even though the noise I want to investigate is coming from out front, I head back to the kitchen to get a bottle of water from my mini dorm fridge.

My first gulp burns, the second gulp going down a bit easier. That's when someone knocks on the kitchen door. Glancing down to the yoga pants and t-shirt I slept in, I wonder if I have enough time to put on a bra. The knock comes again.

I look around and see a flannel button up sitting on top of a box. Setting my water bottle next to it, I quickly pull it on and button it up as I walk over to the kitchen door.

"Hello," I greet, opening it, surprised to see Noah on the other side.

"I need your car keys," he replies, holding out his hand.

What in the world?

"What?" I ask, my forehead wrinkling.

He gestures with his thumb over his shoulder. "Your dumpster is here and your car is blocking the drive."

"They can't be here," I argue. "They were supposed to call first."

All he does is smirk.

Peeking around him I look down my drive and dumbly say. "They're here."

He starts laughing and I turn to glare at him. "They were supposed to call."

Leaving him standing in the open doorway, I grab my keys.

"Where are you going?" He asks, when I go to walk past him.

"To move my car," I reply.

He puts out his palm. "I said I'd move it for you."

"I can move my own car," I snap.

He stops me. "You're barefoot."

I look down at my bare feet before I pass him my keys with a groan. "Fine."

He grins at me. It's too early in the morning for this. What is the dumpster doing here? I mean, I'm happy it's here but they were supposed to call first.

Did they call? My phone is plugged into my charger over by my air mattress. While Noah moves my car and hopefully doesn't steal it, I grab my phone.

One check at the notifications and I realize the trash company not only called, they called four times. That wasn't the most surprising part; it was past nine AM.

I never sleep in this late.

Unless you're sick, I remind myself.

"You need new brakes," Noah mutters from behind me and I jump.

"They called," I reply, lifting my phone as evidence.

He grins again.

Taking my keys, I toss them onto my air mattress. The throw reminds me how sore I am. Reaching up, I massage my shoulder, rolling it.

"Are you okay?" Noah asks.

"I think I slept weird," I reply, rolling it again.

"Could be the mattress." He bumps it with his foot.

It slides across the floor to the center of the room. If he was trying to demonstrate how light it is, he proved his point.

"As soon as I'm done with the floors upstairs, I'll buy a decent one," I say quietly.

My impulse is to be embarrassed. I have money in the bank; I'm only trying to be sensible with my purchases.

"You could stay with me," he says, before pressing his lips together.

I stare at him and then ask, "Why would I do that?"

He walks into the kitchen without answering me. I step into my flip-flops and follow him.

"You didn't answer me."

"I have a spare room in a house where there are no issues with the floors, the walls, or the mattress."

"But you're a stranger," I blurt.

He folds his arms across his broad chest. "Since you just moved here, everyone is."

"You're absolutely right." I shift on my feet, hoping he doesn't sense my nervousness. "Even so, I will be fine here."

There's a loud boom from outside and I hurry past Noah to the door.

"Relax Finley, that's only the dumpster," Noah says.

My steps slow. Oh. I feel silly for rushing.

"Will it hurt my driveway?" I ask.

He comes up close behind me and reaches past me to open my kitchen door for me. "Go see for yourself."

His arm is stretched out over my shoulder, his body heat tickling my senses. This close I can smell his after-shave. It's woodsy with a rich musk, it makes me want to shove my nose into the spot where his shoulder meets his neck and inhale.

Instead, I step out on to my driveway to admire my gigantic and surprisingly expensive trashcan. It's empty now, but I'm going fill it with everything that's wrong with my house so I can rebuild with everything right.

"I have a dumpster," I brag.

Noah chuckles, and I can feel the breath of it on the back of my head. "You sure do."

Turning, I watch the delivery men leave and return their waves.

Spinning back to face Noah I ask, "Should I have tipped them?"

His eyes crinkle with amusement. "No, you don't tip the dumpster delivery company."

Did I seriously just ask if I should tip dumpster delivery people?

He must think I'm an idiot. "Just checking."

"You sure you want to get rid of all the bushes in your front yard?" Noah asks, changing the subject.

"Yes," I clear my throat, suddenly wishing for my water bottle.

"This spray is no joke. It'll kill everything." He says, watching my face.

"No way," I breathe.

"Way," he replies, walking away.

"That's awesome," I reply.

Someday the front of my house will be so pretty it won't need bushes to dress it up. All I want is some grass and a couple of planters for flowers on either side of the front door.

"If you're sure, I'm going to go spray it right now."

"You don't have to," I say, chasing after him. "I can do it."

His eyes move back to my feet. "You're not wearing the right shoes, and since it won't take long, you can get changed while I do it."

He does make a good point. The spray is most likely a harsh chemical to kill the plants the way he said it would. It would not be a good idea to get any of that on my skin. He's wearing rugged boots and work pants.

"Thank you," I murmur and make my way back inside, grinning at my dumpster when I pass it.

I change into a pair of jeans and a tank top before pulling my hair into a ponytail. Makeup is pointless but I do smooth some moisturizer with an SPF on.

Noah is in my den when I walk out of the bathroom, taking the dimensions of the room.

"Thanks again for spraying down the front. It'll be nice when the path to the door isn't a jungle. What are you taking measurements for?"

He straightens and looks me up and down. "Nice boots."

They're steel toe with a fun floral print. My heel turns so I can admire them.

"Thanks," I reply, then repeat my question, "What are you taking measurements for? I thought you were going to look at the furnace?"

"My partner couldn't come by today so I'm going to get you started on pulling up the flooring while I go pick up plywood for your new subfloor instead." Then he pauses, his eyes roaming over my face. "As long as you're feeling up to starting today."

"I am." I reply.

He crosses the den and moves into the kitchen. "I got you these."

I follow him, stopping when he picks up a plastic bag. He turns, offering the bag to me. What on earth?

Taking it, I stare at him instead of reaching into the

bag like a normal person. "Why are you doing all of this?"

He pushes his hands into his pockets. "All of what?"

"You've sprayed down my front yard." I lift the bag. "Got me something, and you said you were going to get plywood. I don't know how much you've spent already and you haven't said anything about how much the plywood will be."

His mouth twitches. "How about you look and see what I got you before you freak."

With a frown, I open the bag, and then I feel silly. In it is a pair of teal work gloves and matching kneepads. In all my planning, getting a pair of thick work gloves and kneepads was something I had forgotten.

I lift my eyes to his. "These are really nice. Thank you."

"The gloves and kneepads are a gift, and not an expensive one so you don't need to feel obligated and like I told you yesterday, the spray was my brother's. He didn't charge me for it. Plywood isn't expensive and even if it was, there's no getting around needing it for your floors."

I bend my knees to set the bag on the floor and straighten, lifting my hands up in surrender. "No, you're right. I'm sorry I panicked. I'm still getting used to the idea of having help. Should I go with you to get the wood, so I can pay for it?"

He shakes his head. "We can settle up later. You can work on the floors while I'm gone."

I grimace. "It's cool that I eat first, right?"

He nods, lifting his hand to scratch the back of his head. "Of course. Do you want me to pick you up something?"

I shake my head. "I have stuff here."

What I don't tell him is it's a bulk size box of breakfast

bars.

"Do you need any tips on how to rip up the flooring?"

I shrug. "I'm not sure."

The existing flooring is in such bad shape there are patches where it's already coming up on its own.

He passes me a small crowbar. "Do what you can and I'll help as soon as I'm back with the wood. Start in the far corner of the den and make sure to wear the gloves."

"I will," I promise.

He leaves and I can't help it, my eyes are drawn to him as I watch him go. Even though he's almost the opposite of Allen in every way, I'm still pissed at myself for being attracted to him. The last thing I want or need is a new man in my life, especially not one who buys condoms by the truckload. Would it kill him to have a humpback instead of broad shoulders and an ass you could bounce a quarter off of?

Day one and he's already helped so much. Yesterday he said I'd be the boss but he seems to be the only one making decisions so far. I decide against calling him out on it because I have no idea what I'm doing here.

Wanting to have progress to show by the time he's back, I scarf down my breakfast and get to work. The wood flooring comes up easily. Piling it up on my wheelbarrow, I make multiple trips out to the dumpster. The pieces that I'm pulling up are hardwood planks laid out in a parquet pattern, which means each piece I pull up isn't big or heavy. I'm grateful for both but the process is beyond tedious and on my hands and knees, I'm definitely starting to feel it in my shoulders.

I ignore the ache; I never assumed this project would be easy. With each plank I pull, I'm getting stronger.

What I can't figure out how to get up is the existing

subfloor. There are parts that show signs of rot but without a saw I can't pull them up by hand.

Focusing on the floor, I can keep my progress going. I'm a good ways toward the middle of the room by the time Noah gets back. He unloads large sheets of plywood into the front living room before coming to check on me.

"Not bad," he says, his voice full of pride.

I wipe some sweat from my brow. "I couldn't figure out how to pull up the bottom part."

He hands me a bottle of water. "We'll have to use a saw to do that."

We work together for the next hour. When Noah isn't looking, I watch him. I tell myself it's to appreciate how efficiently he moves. For every plank I pull up, he pulls up four. He does use a larger crow bar but his skill is still undeniable. The truth is, I'm captivated by the power he displays, the way his muscles flex and bulge with his movements.

"Do I have something on my ass?"

My eyes snap to his face and I stutter, "I-I w-wasn't looking at your ass."

He hums.

"I wasn't," I say more firmly this time.

He grins at me. "Okay."

I try not to look at him anymore but it's impossible. He's too attractive, it would be a disservice not to.

We've worked all morning and have all of the planks from the den pulled up and thrown into the dumpster.

"Time to start on the existing subfloor," he says after taking out the last batch of rotted wood planks.

"Be careful," I warn.

He grins at me. "Come over here. I'll show you how

it's done."

There's a spot in the corner that is rotten straight through. He starts there, and I move to crouch next to him. He points out where he plans to make the cuts so he can avoid the jousts below it.

He cuts out a small square first, and with a grunt, pulls it up.

"This is good," he says, pointing to the wood beneath it. "Look. The rot doesn't seem to have spread beyond the floor and subfloor."

He pulls a screwdriver from his belt and jabs at the jousts to show me how solid they are.

"That's great!" I beam.

He blinks at me before looking back down at the jousts, a small smile tugging at the corners of his mouth.

The condition of this house wasn't a surprise. I knew I was buying it as is. My home inspector assured me that the foundation, beams and jousts were all sound. It's a relief to get confirmation of that. I was terrified I'd open up the floor and find a rotted disaster.

"How long do you think it will take to get all of this up?" I ask.

"You should move your fridge and microwave to one of the front rooms and keep pulling up the flooring into the kitchen. I'll get as much of this up as I can before I have to leave."

"You have to leave?" I ask, and then feel silly for it.

Of course he has to leave. It's already insane that he's helping me at all.

He leans back, resting his forearm against his knee. His gaze is intense.

"I can come back tonight. We can eat and then keep working."

"You'd do that?" I ask, and then add, "come back and help me?"

"Try and keep me away," he murmurs, holding my gaze.

I look away first, biting back a smile as I get back to work. When I turn back to see how Noah's doing, my jaw drops.

I gasp and feel my eyes widen. "Wow! You move fast."

He gives me a half grin. "This isn't my first time."

Wow that sounded flirty. Would it be insane to flirt back? Then I remember I'm still sick, not wearing makeup, and am covered in dirt and sweat.

Not to mention the fact that I've decided I should be on my own for the time being. I'm clearly reading too much into how nice he is.

Sticking with gratitude, I look at him, hoping he believes what I'm about to say. "Thank you again for doing this."

"You're welcome." He gives me a smile, and we both get back to work.

By the time I have the old wooden planks up in the kitchen, he has the new subfloor down in the den.

When he finishes that, he helps me break apart and toss the old cabinetry.

"That's all I can do for now."

"All?" I laugh, looking at everything we've done in only part of a day. "You've done so much."

He wets his lips and I hurriedly offer him a bottle of water.

Taking it from me, he says, "I'll be back later with dinner. Try to rest up so you'll be ready to work."

Gesturing toward the wood planks now uncovered

from where the cabinetry was I ask, "Should I finish pulling those up?"

He nods. "Go for it."

I do, working until the cable guy shows up.

He gives me a dubious look as I usher him inside. One good thing about all the holes in my walls from the new electrical wiring is the cable guy doesn't need to make any new ones. While he works, I finish pulling up the planks in the kitchen.

I'm finished before he is. Though I'm tempted to, I don't attempt to pull up any of the subflooring. Instead, I admire my new plywood subfloor in the den. Once the cable guy is done, I stop daydreaming about wood flooring and hook up my computer and TV.

After that, I call my mom to share all my good news.

"And he's doing it all out of the goodness of his own heart?" She asks after I tell her about Noah.

"His sister is my realtor Abby," I explain.

She hmpfs on her end of the line. "I never had the sibling of a realtor renovate any of our houses and we moved four times before we bought this house."

"Okay, I get this isn't something that happens everyday but he was concerned I took on more than I could handle."

"Your father and I were concerned and you wouldn't let us help," she argues.

"Mom," I warn. "I thought this was good news, I wouldn't have told you if I thought it would upset you."

"Finley Elizabeth Reeves, don't you dare say you'd ever keep things from me,"

"Yes, mama," I agree readily.

"Well, tell me about this man. What does he look like?"

"Why does that matter?" I ask defensively.

My mom covers the mouth of the phone to say something to my dad; too bad I hear every single word. "She won't tell me what he looks like so that means he's good looking."

CHAPTER 6

Noah

FROM FINLEY'S HOUSE I drive home to shower and change before my appointment. While I am a contractor, I doubt showing up filthy and soaked with sweat will inspire anyone to hire us.

More than once, after leaving her, Finley drifts into my thoughts. We worked well together. She's strong and didn't expect me to do all of the work even though I offered to help. She also made a point to bring up paying me back for the plywood.

I've known women who have no problem being taken care of. I appreciate the fact that Finley isn't like that. Hell, she's sick and is still working her ass off.

My phone rings while I drive. Since I show up early to my appointment I have time to check my message.

It's Eli, being his usual overbearing and bossy self. Someone, probably Abby, told him about Finley and the work I'm doing on her house given the fact that in his message he asks if I've lost my mind doing free work for a woman I've just met.

I decide against calling him back. If I do, we'll probably argue and I'll say things I'll regret. With everything he has going on with Brooke, I'm not surprised he's calling me. He's got to be pretty pissed at life and he's taking it out on me. I didn't ask for, nor do I need his opinion.

The only opinion that truly matters is Jon's since I was at her house during work hours. As long as he's cool with what I'm doing, that's all I need. He's a romantic and he's got Emily involved so I could spend every day for the next month there and he wouldn't care.

Now, all I have to do is have a word with Abby to encourage her to keep her mouth shut in the future, not that she'll listen to me. I send her a text anyway.

Then I get to work. This appointment is more successful than the one yesterday. They hire us to take down an interior wall and redo the flooring in that room.

It's a solid job for clients we've worked with before. We also have other previous clients that live on their street. Our trucks have our logo on them and we normally pick up repeat business when other homeowners see us in the area.

I can make sure Jon has some extra business cards on him. He can have one of the guys stick them behind the metal flags on the mailboxes of the street they're working on.

I head back to the office and am surprised to find Abby waiting for me. I expected a response of some sort to my text. She meets me at the door of my truck.

"Don't you have a job?" I joke.

"I got a new listing earlier and had a client make an offer on a condo today. Don't worry about my job, I'm kicking serious realtor ass at the moment. Now, what'd Eli say to you?" She asks.

"He alluded to me being an idiot who thinks with his dick for the work I'm doing at Fin's house," I reply, holding open the door for her.

"Typical Eli," she mutters.

"Hey Justin," I wave, once we're inside.

He lifts his chin and replies, "Noah, Abigail."

After I close the door to my office behind us I ask, "Abigail?"

She laughs. "I think I intimidate him."

"Don't mess with his head," I order. She rolls her eyes. "Now, why were you talking about me with Eli?"

She settles herself into one of the chairs across from my desk and then shifts in it, trying to get comfortable. I have very comfortable chairs so it's answering my question that must be bothering her.

"Abby," I grunt.

She crosses her arms over her chest. "It just came out. I'm sorry."

"How does what I'm doing just come out?" I question.

Her arms fall to either side of the chair. "I was trying to get him to open up about Brooke so I told him you were interested in someone and how you were helping her out."

Slumping into my chair I groan. "Why?"

"I know," she replies. "I'm sorry. I never would have told him if I thought he would lay into you about it."

"Can you please keep my personal shit to yourself going forward?" I ask.

She nods. "I will. I promise but, Gideon knows, too, and that wasn't my fault."

"I told him," I explain.

She folds her arms across her chest as she cocks her

head to the side. "If you're telling people, why can't I tell people?"

I love my sister. I want to strangle her every once and a while, like right now, but I do love her.

"Maybe because it's my information to share," I counter.

That derails her and she nods. "Did you go over there today?"

I nod.

"Well," she presses when I don't give her any more information. "What happened?"

"Nothing," I reply, deciding against telling her I'm going back over there tonight.

"That's all?" She asks. "You didn't start working on it or anything?"

"We pulled up the flooring in the kitchen and den and got new subflooring down in the den."

She blinks. "You did all of that today?"

I shrug. She grins.

"I'm still pissed at you."

Her smile falls. "I deserve that."

Seeing her upset is harder than being angry at her. "Alright. You're forgiven." I point at her. "As long as you don't do it again."

She holds up her hands. "I won't. I promise. My lips are sealed when it comes to you and Finley. Side note, when did you start calling her Fin?"

Damn it.

"She told me her friends called her that," I explain, hoping I'm not giving too much away.

"When are you seeing her again?" She asks.

"Don't worry about it," I grunt. "Did Eli tell you

anymore about what's going on with him and Brooke?"

She frowns. "You're seriously not telling me?"

I shake my head and she huffs.

"I told him I'm taking the kids to a movie this week. He wanted to meet me but I don't want them telling Brooke and her thinking I was trying to play her. That pissed him off, but whatever. I don't want his bullshit to keep me from seeing my niece and nephews if they end up getting a divorce."

"How did he take that?" I ask.

Eli has never taken hearing the word no well.

"He was pissed but he doesn't scare me."

She's lucky he's never unleashed the full power of his wrath on her. If he had, she'd be more concerned about him being pissed.

"Good for you."

She smirks. It couldn't have been easy growing up with four brothers. There are plenty of times we drove her crazy. She learned early on how to hold her own.

"We done here?" I ask.

"You're really not going to tell me anything?" She argues.

"And have you tell everyone?" I counter.

She stands, slinging her purse over her shoulder. "I'll just find out from Finley."

"Go for it," I reply.

Her brows furrow. "You're so annoying."

I grin. "I love you too."

She stomps out of my office. It's crazy how that never gets old.

"Your sister offered me a hundred bucks to key your truck," Justin calls out a minute after she's gone.

"Hold out for two hundred!"

When he doesn't say anything I assume he took my advice.

A few hours later, once I'm ready to leave, I text Finley to let her know I'm on the way. I pick up food near her house so it'll still be hot by the time I get there.

She's waiting for me in her driveway. The outside light above her kitchen door is on and she's set up a bistro table and two chairs.

"Fancy," I tease.

She rests her chin on her palm. "Thanks. It was a moving present from my parents."

I set the takeout bag onto the table. "I hope Chinese is okay."

"I love Chinese," she replies and then stands. "What would you like to drink? I have wine, or bottled water."

I'm typically more of a beer guy but enjoy a glass of wine every now and then, and it might take the edge off a bit if we both have one. "Wine, thanks."

She walks into her house and returns quickly with two glasses. I lean back in my chair and take a drink. There's nothing like a New England summer evening. It's perfect now, but if we stay out once the sun goes down we'll get eaten alive by mosquitos. Since there's work to do, we'll be inside long before they'll be able to make a feast of us.

While we eat, I try to get to know her better.

"What made you decide to move here?"

Her eyes shift away. "It's a long story."

"We have plenty of time," I counter.

"Parts of it will sound silly," she argues.

She moved cross-country, to renovate a house in a

state she's never lived in all by herself. Silly isn't the word I would think of. "You can tell me anything."

She nods. "I needed a change. I love my family but I needed to get away so I could have a fresh start. The silly part is I could have ended up anywhere. I was waiting to find a house that spoke to me."

My gaze moves to the kitchen door. "And this one did."

She nods her head. "When I saw the listing online I knew this was the place I was meant to live."

"Why?"

She gulps. "It's going to sound crazy."

I shrug. "Try me."

"Well, not all of it is crazy," she amends, and explains. "The price and location were both right. I looked at hundreds of houses but this one was different. With this house," her face softens as her eyes move from mine to her house, "it stopped being all about getting away. When I looked at the pictures online I could already imagine what it would look like when it was finished."

"Abby says that happens all the time with the houses she shows. That when a house speaks to a client they know it's the one to make an offer on."

"Yes, this house spoke to me." Her eyes are bright. "Thanks for not thinking I'm crazy for wanting to fix up this place."

"It's not crazy to want to fix something."

She passes me a fortune cookie and then starts to open the other one. I watch as she breaks it in half and tugs the paper fortune free. Her lips tip up as she reads it.

"What does it say?"

She tilts her head to my unopened cookie. "You first."

Shaking my head, I don't argue that her fortune is already out. Once I have it open, my eyes move across the text. *There is no fear for the one whose thought is not confused.*

"Well." Impatience coats her words. "Read it."

I press the paper to my chest. "Why should I?"

She reaches across the table, her hand wrapping around my wrist. "I want to see."

Her skin is soft and smooth, not yet marred with calluses from work.

Her fortune sits face up in front of her. She lets go of my wrist to grab it when she notices my eyes on it. Instantly, I miss the feel of her touch.

Slowly rising from my chair, I take a step towards her. She twists out of her chair and moves to stand behind it, a wild grin on her face. Who knew fighting over fortune cookie fortunes could be this fun?

"If you run, I'll catch you," I taunt.

She laughs. "Maybe it will be me chasing you."

That's something I'd like to see.

"You'd never be able to catch me."

She wets her lips. "I had the school record for the mile in elementary school."

Dropping back into my seat I laugh and then hand her my fortune. "Okay Flash. Here you go."

She punches the air to celebrate her victory before taking my fortune, her fingertips brushing against mine as she does. Her sensuous lips move as she reads it.

When she's done reading she says, "That's a good one."

"Are you going to tell me yours?"

She's still holding hers and keeps mine, putting it

behind her fortune. "Be patient. The Great Wall of China wasn't built in a day." She holds my gaze as she slips both scraps of paper into her pocket. "Does that mean we should stop for the night?"

Turning my gaze, I look at our empty food containers. "Not a chance. Break's over. Time to get back to work."

We quickly clean up, tossing our trash right into her dumpster. Then I follow her into the house, liking the fact that she carried my fortune with her.

"I got my cable set up today," she brags, showing me her set up.

"That's good." I give her a website address to look up. "If you pick floors from here I can get them at cost. This site will show you everything we have in stock."

"*You* have in stock? Do you sell flooring?" Her brows knit together in confusion as she studies my face.

I scratch the back of my head. "I don't sell it, but my family does."

Her mouth falls open. "Your family sells flooring?"

I nod, "And plywood, and drywall, and shingles, and well, you get the idea. My family owns a hardware store. If it's home related, they sell it."

"It's like you're my fairy home building Godmother," she teases.

My face twists. "Godmother?"

She covers her mouth to muffle a laugh. "Sorry. Godfather."

I give her my best Brando, stroking my chin. "I can handle Godfather." She smiles at me in return, causing me to stare at her mouth. I clear my throat. "So, you see any floors you like?"

She turns back to her computer and starts to excitedly scroll and click through the pictures. "I like this one. Oh and this one! And what do you think about this one?"

I move to stand behind her. Instead of a desk, she has both her TV and laptop sitting on a folding card table. She points out her three top choices to me.

"The thing to remember about a dark wood floor is that it shows everything, including every speck of dust."

Her nose wrinkles. "I'm not a fan of dusting everyday."

I point to her next choice. "This flooring is sturdy and will hold up well over time."

"I like the sound of that." She nods, still looking at the screen.

Then I point to her last choice. "This one is my favorite of the three. I have it installed in my house if you'd like to check it out in person."

She gulps. "Go to your house?"

I shrug, taking a step back. "I did say you could stay in my spare room if you'd like."

She's shaking her head before I even finish speaking. "I don't think that would be a good idea."

Unable to stop myself, I ask, "Why not?"

"I don't know what to think of you. This all seems crazy, everything that you've done already and are still doing for me."

"I don't mind."

She doesn't seem convinced. "Have you ever done this before? Is rescuing damsels in renovation distress your thing?"

"My thing? No, I've never done anything like this."

She pushes away from her computer. "What am I supposed to think? I don't want to look a gift horse in the mouth—"

I cut her off. "So what if it isn't normal. Is moving cross country to a place you've never even visited before normal?"

She frowns.

Deciding to stop before I push too far, I shift the conversation back to the floors. "If you like the flooring on the website I can order whichever one you want."

"Fine," she says, not looking at me. "I like the last one the best. It's exactly what I pictured in my head."

"I'll find out tomorrow if they have all you need in stock. Do you want the same flooring in the front rooms?"

She nods, standing. Since I already have her measurements, it'll be easy to put the order in.

"I want it to all match." Her head turns as her gaze moves across the room.

"What is your vision?" I ask, kicking myself for not asking her sooner.

"What?" She breathes.

I gesture to the room around us. "The other day you said you could picture this place all done. Walk me through it. What's your dream?"

She smiles shyly, her gaze again moving across the room. "Simple, clean, and comfortable. I want the walls and floors to be neutral so I can change out colors with rugs and throw pillows whenever I want."

"What about your kitchen?" I ask, my head tilting toward the doorway.

She walks to the kitchen and I follow her as she points to each spot as she explains her vision. "I want a deep farmhouse sink, and an over-sized refrigerator." She moves around the small area and stands with her hands out next to her. "The gas stove will go here and I want this area for prep with the dishwasher under it."

As she describes her perfect kitchen, her entire face lights up with excitement. All I can do is stare.

"Do you like to cook?"

She smiles outright. "I love to cook."

"What color cabinets do you want?" I ask, positive that she not only knows but probably has a picture of her dream kitchen either in her mind or saved on her computer.

"White shaker style lower cabinets and glass front upper cabinets."

Knew it.

"Backsplash?"

"White subway tiles," she replies without waiting a beat.

"A classic," I agree. "It'll look great once we put it all in."

Her face softens. "Is there anything you can't do?"

I decide against giving her a list of my failings and instead tell her, "If I think of something I'll let you know."

She stares at me, long enough for me to worry if I have something on my face.

"I told my mother about you," she says, surprising me.

I swallow hard. "And what did you say?"

"I told her you were helping me with the house."

Somehow, I know she's not telling me everything.

"What was her reaction?"

She shrugs. "She was happy I had help but was concerned about your motives."

"My motives," I repeat.

She nods.

Truth is, she *should* be worried about my motives. She wants to relax in front of her fire in her fixed up house and I want her in my bed.

She waits for me to say something more, maybe even to come clean about why I'm really doing this.

I'm smarter than that. "Did you tell her all the progress you've made?"

She blinks at my subject change and then nods her head. "I did and I told her I'd never have managed it without you."

"I disagree. You could and would have done this. It would have taken longer, but that isn't a surprise if you were working alone. Many hands make light work."

"You give me too much credit."

My praise is making her uncomfortable so to change the subject, I say the first thing that I think of. "Tell me about your ex-husband."

Her mouth falls open and she walks away.

"Fin!" I call, following her.

"We've been doing too much talking when we should have been working."

It's clearly too soon to ask about her husband.

"I'm sorry I pried."

She waves me off and straps on her kneepads. "It's fine. Should I grab a new sheet of plywood while you saw this part?"

Seems the conversation portion of our evening has ended and the manual labor part has begun.

"Sounds good."

Any communication between us for the next two hours is limited to me giving directions and her accepting them. Each and every attempt I make to steer our conversation back toward anything else, she shuts down.

Her ex must have done a number on her for her to be this tight lipped on the subject. That, or she was the one in the wrong and is dealing with guilt. Could this house and all the work she plans to do to it be some kind of self-imposed penance?

"Can you press down right here?" I ask, pointing to one corner of the subfloor.

She moves, kneeling where I asked and pressing down to help hold the wood in place. My gaze travels over her and I freeze. The way she's bent, I can see right down her shirt. My eyes drink her in until I manage to tear them away. This may be the most painful renovation of my life.

CHAPTER 7

Finley

"THANK YOU. HAVE a nice day, sir." I press end on the call and quickly change my call status from available to offline. My shift is officially over for the day, and now the real work begins. Leaning forward, I pull my headphones off and set them next to my computer then I reach down to turn off my heating pad.

Over the past two weeks, Noah has been over almost every night after work and on the weekends. My new subfloors are done and we've pulled off all the drywall on the first floor, including the ceiling. There were a few places where we needed, and by we, I mean Noah, to repair some wood rot in the walls.

Then we used this machine to blow foam insulation into the spaces between the studs. Tonight we start putting up new drywall. Noah says the walls need to be up and primed before we install my new wood floors.

This whole time I've also been back to work during the day. I'm currently in a near constant state of sore.

Working on this house, I've discovered muscles I was

not aware existed. All of my aches and pains have the happy side effect of keeping my thoughts squarely on the physical. If by some chance they drift to Allen, all I have to do is *try* and lift my hand above my head to focus on the pain instead.

More than once, Noah has offered me his spare bedroom. Each and every time I've declined. I can't spend the night at his house. That would be bonkers, or at least crazier than my current level of insane.

Last week I bought another queen-size air mattress that I stacked on top of the one I already had. As long as I keep them both full of air it's almost like I'm sleeping on a regular bed. At least that's what I keep telling myself each time I wake up after toppling off of one in the middle of the night to stop daydreaming about any of the beds in his house.

The one daydream that I've been unable to stop, though, is the one where I throw myself at Noah.

Yesterday he took off his shirt.

He's so broad and solid and I could not stop staring at his chest hair.

What is wrong with me?

I had a plan. My plan didn't include a hot contractor helping me, but since I'm weeks ahead of schedule and under budget I'm not complaining.

I'm still a mess. This morning, my social media account showed me a memory that on this day seven years ago Allen and I went to Las Vegas. It was the last time I remembered being happy in my marriage. Not just that, it was the last time I felt any sort of hope for our future.

Looking at myself in that picture, the weight of the last seven years came crashing down on me. I cried through my lunch break and sniffled off and on through my afternoon calls.

Noah will be here any minute and I'm sure he'll know I've been crying. Why am I even crying over Allen? He was a mediocre boyfriend who became an awful husband. I should be jumping up and down and singing freedom at the top of my lungs. He doesn't deserve my tears and it's seriously pissing me off that he got them.

"Finley, you here?"

I plaster on a fake smile. "I sure am."

He sets a toolbox down. "I have a surprise for you."

That gets my attention. I stand, groaning as I do.

"Your back hurting?" He asks, his expression not masking his concern.

"Just stiff. I'll be fine once I'm moving around so no changing the subject. What's the surprise?"

His eyes move over me, examining me with his gaze as I close the distance between us. "Your eyes are puffy and your nose is red. Have you been crying?"

I frown, glaring at him. "It's from the construction dust. It's been making my eyes water and me sneeze all day."

His eyes narrow as he considers my words. Can he tell I'm lying?

My answer is completely plausible. We've been kicking up tons of dust, not that any of it has made me sneeze. It might sound crazy but I don't mind the mess. It's proof of all the progress we've made and luck that we've been able to do the work at all.

"Surprise?" I remind him.

He frowns but does it holding open the door for me. "Check out what's in the trailer."

The trailer? He only hitches it to his truck when whatever he's hauling won't fit in the bed. There's only one thing I've ordered recently that wouldn't fit.

I grab his arm, my chest pounding when I feel how firm it is. "Is it?"

He nods and I give him a grin before racing out the door. Since we raked up all the carcasses of the jungle that once made up my front walkway impassable, it's easier to maneuver around and makes it actually usable. Not to mention it looks like less of a dump. I skid to a stop at the back of Noah's trailer and open the doors.

"My floors!" I exclaim, turning to grin up at Noah who followed me out to his truck. "Does this mean we get to start them tonight?"

They did not have the wood floors I wanted in stock. I had assumed Noah said we needed to do the walls first to keep me distracted until they came.

He shakes his head. "We still need to drywall first."

"But why?" I interrupt, gesturing to the trailer full of hardwood.

"We need to unload the flooring and let it acclimate to the climate of your house," he explains.

I gape at him and can't help but argue. "That sounds made up."

He reaches past me to pull a box out, motioning with his head for me to grab the other end. "It's not."

"Bummer," I say, my lower lip pushing out.

He takes one hand from the box to give my hand a gentle squeeze. "No pouting. You get new walls today."

The shock of his callused fingers on my skin makes me shiver. To hide my reaction, and since I can't argue with his logic, I pull away to grab the other end of the box.

My voice sounds funny when I ask. "How was your day?"

His head tilts to the side. If he heard the strain in my voice he doesn't mention it. "Annoying but better now."

Better now?

I avoid that and focus on the first thing he said. "Annoying how?"

"Eli," he grunts.

He doesn't mention his older brother often, but when he does it's clear they clash. "What happened?"

"He was there when I picked up the floors."

"I'm sorry," I whisper.

He blinks at me. "You're apologizing for my brother being an ass?"

I shrug.

He reaches out and tugs on my ponytail. "Thanks."

Unloading a million boxes of wood flooring sucks. The first one we carried didn't feel that heavy. The fortieth one on the other hand, weighs a friggin' ton. What doesn't suck is the way his biceps look each time he lifts one.

We split them up across the four main rooms because Noah claims that the climate from one room can differ to another. We break for water before getting started on the walls.

We've got all the drywall up in the kitchen when I ask, "Time for dinner?"

Noah uses his forearm to wipe sweat from his forehead. "I could eat."

"What sounds good? I can go grab it."

His face softens. "Only if you let me pay."

This has become our nightly dance. I offer to get food, and Noah accepts as long as he gets to pay. I would argue that he had already paid and that he was doing all this free labor on top of that. He would then counter that once we put in my kitchen he'd be willing to let me cook for him.

My love for cooking and excitement over designing a kitchen had come out last week. I'm not sure if he believes that I'm an excellent cook or not.

"Fine," I grumble, holding out my hand.

Before he can pull out his wallet, we hear a giant crash from the back of the house.

With wide eyes I gasp, "What was that?"

He turns, charging toward the hall. What he doesn't do is answer me. I chase after him, trying to overtake him but a muscled arm holds me back.

When we reach the opening to the den and kitchen, my lips part in shock. The arm holding me back becomes the anchor I cling to so I don't collapse to the floor. I'm not sure where to look first, to the gaping hole in my ceiling or at the shattered toilet in front of us.

"Is that my toilet?" I stupidly ask.

"Yep."

My eyes move back to the ceiling. "There's a giant hole in my ceiling."

"Yep."

I huff out a breath. "Can you say anything other than yep?"

His head turns so he can grin down at me. Growling, I smack his arm before he can say yep again.

"What am I going to do?" I ask, my voice rising with my panic.

He moves, so fast that if I had blinked I would have missed it. Standing so close, his head dips, his lips inches from mine. A toilet just fell through my ceiling and I think Noah is about to kiss me. I so cannot handle that right now. Ducking his embrace I dash around him, the porcelain wreckage on the floor my excuse.

"I'm in over my head," I admit, for multiple reasons.

He exhales and I cringe, cringe right down to my bones. What is my problem, apart from the obvious?

"I'm guessing you don't want to add a bathroom right here?" His voice is full of humor.

Some of my embarrassment floats away on the wings of the unexpected laughter that bubbles up inside of me.

Pointing at the mess I continue the laugh. "There's a toilet in my den."

He stands next to me and I follow his gaze to the ceiling. "Another couple of holes and you could have a skylight."

We both laugh and I'm grateful there isn't any uncomfortable tension still lingering between us.

Because of that I feel safe enough to repeat my earlier question. "What am I going to do?"

"First, you're going to take a deep breath. Then, you're going to remember that either of us could have been standing under it when it fell. Last, we're going to go upstairs to see how bad the floors are rotted."

Turning, I blink up into his ocean blue eyes and reply, "I wanted to reuse that toilet in my new bathroom."

His warm gaze travels over my face. "You're gonna need a new one."

I glumly nod in agreement.

I follow him up the stairs to see the rest of the damage. "Does stuff like this happen a lot in renovations?"

He glances over his shoulder. "Yep."

I frown at his back but keep my mouth shut. I'm not

sure how much wiggle room my budget has for another disaster. He makes me stay at the top of the stairs, the only part of the second floor he's certain isn't rotted, while he looks at the floors.

"What do I do if you fall through too?" I ask, only half joking.

"Call 911."

Such a smart ass, that one.

His response makes my heart start wildly thumping in my chest. "Maybe we should have someone else look at the floors."

His head pops out of the guest bath. "Worried about me?"

I shrug, avoiding his eyes.

Carefully stepping out of the bathroom, he says, "Gutting that room just turned into a priority. Wait there while I check the master."

Holding myself still, I focus all my attention on listening to his steps, cringing each time the floor groans or squeaks beneath them.

When he makes his way back to me I almost sag with relief. "How bad is it?"

Gesturing over his shoulder with his thumb he explains, "there's water damage but not as bad as the guest bath." He's standing right next to me, so close his breath tickles my cheek when he adds, "your other toilet is safe to reuse."

"Hooray," I manage to squeak out and then want to kick myself.

Who celebrates saving a toilet? Apparently I do.

He follows me down the stairs and together we clean up the mess in the den. The water damage upstairs isn't a surprise and thankfully, since the flow had been turned off up there, the mess we cleared wasn't a wet one.

After our last load to the dumpster, Noah pulls out his wallet. "I was hungry before. Now I'm starving."

"You're already doing so much. The least I could do is buy you dinner," I argue.

He holds out a couple of bills to me. His smile does not fade when I grumble how stubborn he is.

"And take my truck," he orders.

I roll my eyes but don't fight him. After he heard my brakes he started making me use his Chevy. He got me an appointment with his mechanic for later this week.

Besides, driving his truck is fun. My dad has one a lot like it and he never let me drive it. I also like what it says about how Noah feels about me. I mean, aren't men supposedly notoriously protective of their vehicles? I like that he trusts me with it.

My eyes move to my house before I pull away. Being the last house on a dead end street gives the illusion that my house isn't in a city. It's not downtown or anything but there is still a great selection of restaurants. I drive to a burger place and order easily for both of us. It's crazy, I've known Noah less than a month but I already know so much about him, if knowing what someone would order from multiple places counts.

When I get back to the house with our food, I'm pleasantly surprised to see Abby's car. She's checking out the hole in my ceiling when I come in.

"Hey Finley," she greets, walking over to hug me.

"Hi Abby." I give her a one armed hug. "I wish I knew you were coming. I would have gotten you something too," I add, lifting the food bag as explanation.

She shrugs. "I ate before I came and," she gestures to her jogging shorts and t-shirt. "I've come to work."

The couple of times that I've seen her she has always been dressed to the nines. Now here she is in workout clothes, her long light brown hair up in a messy bun, to help me. My mouth falls open and my nose starts stinging for some reason. "Really?"

She grins. "You guys eat while I check out all the work you've done."

After Noah and my first dinner, I moved the bistro table and chairs into the house. Luckily, I set it up in one of the front rooms. Noah and I both settle around it.

"It's amazing how much better this place already looks, apart from the giant hole in the ceiling," Abby says as she explores. "Especially the front yard." Then she tilts her head toward Noah and asks. "Did Gideon clear it?"

Noah sets his burger down and leans back in his chair. "You know he gave me the stuff to do it."

She shrugs and then looks at me. "If he ever sees this place in person he's going to want to do your landscaping."

I have to cover my mouth to hurriedly finish my bite before I ask, "Why?"

"He loves these old houses."

"Who doesn't?" Noah queries.

Noah has made it clear he enjoys working on historic homes.

"It must run in the family," I say.

He surprises me by reaching across the table to smooth the pad of his thumb across the corner of my mouth. "Mustard," he says, showing me his thumb. "And, I love them more."

He then shocks the hell out of me by bringing his thumb to his mouth and licking my mustard from it.

Holy crap, he just licked my mustard.

"You okay?" He asks, breaking my trance.

He caught me staring at his mouth.

Nodding, I gulp then grab my napkin to dab at my mouth in case he didn't get it all. I don't respond verbally to Noah's words, other than the bloom of warmth within my chest.

Abby grins at both of us before walking over to one of the piles of wood flooring. "Love this shade. These will look amazing once they're installed."

"Thank you," I beam.

Once Noah and I are finished eating, the three of us get to work. It's clear that Abby is no slouch when it comes to hanging drywall. I end up helping her by holding up pieces for her to screw in while Noah tackles the guest bath.

Each time he lumbers down the stairs with a load of debris I cringe. "Are you sure you don't need any help?"

"Nope, I've got this," he replies.

Two hours later almost all the drywall for the back half of the house, minus the ceilings, is up and Noah has gutted the upstairs bathroom.

"We'll start the front rooms tomorrow," Noah suggests.

The progress is good but since it hurts like hell to lift my arms, I'm not looking forward to more work.

Abby gives me a limp hug. "You two have fun with that. I'm going home to take a long hot bath."

I sag. "I would kill for a bath."

Abby gets a mischievous look in her eyes before saying, "Noah has this incredible soaking tub at his house." She smacks his arm. "You should let Finley use it some time."

I've been out of high school for close to two decades

but that does not stop me from blushing at her suggestion.

I lift my hands, "Oh, no, no, no. I'm fine. Really."

Noah stares at me, raising his eyebrows. "I don't mind."

A toilet crashed through my ceiling today, now I pray for an anvil to do the same and put me out of my misery.

When I don't reply, Noah continues. "No arguments, you're coming home with me tonight."

"No, I'm not," I grumble.

"Yes, you are," he argues. "You're going to take a bath and sleep in a real bed tonight."

Abby's gaze moves back and forth between us like a spectator watching a tennis match.

"I appreciate the gesture but it's unnecessary. I'm perfectly fine here."

"I know you're fine here, but there's nothing wrong with accepting help when it's offered," he counters.

I fling my hands out to the sides. "What do you call all of this?" I gesture to the room around us. "You've already done too much. I already feel like I'm taking advantage of you."

"Are we friends?"

I frown. That wasn't a fair question to ask. I liked him. Even when I was in stranger danger mode I liked him. He's annoyingly stubborn but it's hard to hold that against him when what he's been so stubborn about was helping me.

When I left Texas, I did it mainly friendless. See, when I found out the people I thought were my friends knew my husband was cheating on me, they stopped being my friends.

I didn't plan on making new ones here. My ability to

trust anyone outside my family was broken, or so I thought. Abby is a sweetheart, but it's Noah who day after day is slowly earning my trust. We are friends or at least I hoped we are.

"Yes," I whisper.

He nods. "So pack a bag."

Abby moves closer to me and pats my arm. "He's right you know. A night away from here would be good for you."

Great, two against one.

My eyes lock with Noah's blue ones. "Are you sure about this?"

"I wouldn't have offered if I wasn't."

I pull in a deep breath, and then nod.

"I'm going to take off," Abby says, giving me a sympathetic smile.

Noah loads his equipment back into his trailer while I pack a bag. I don't have much but whatever valuables I do have, I pack up along with everything I'll need for the night.

"I'm ready," I reply, after locking up.

He comes over to me, taking my duffle bag from me. "Don't sound so excited."

"I don't mean to be difficult when you're being so nice," I reply, annoyed at myself.

He loads my duffle into the back of the trailer before closing and securing its doors. I watch as he reattaches the trailer to the hitch of his truck.

It's like watching him hang drywall all over again. There's no wasted movement. He is so methodical and controlled in his motions. It would have easily taken me twice as long to do it.

"You're good with your hands," I blurt.

When the implication of my words sinks in, my eyes widen. "I mean you're good at the things that you do."

He grins. "Yes, I am."

I decide to keep my mouth shut for the foreseeable future to avoid saying anything else stupid.

Since I'm bone tired, he offers to drive, promising it'll be no big deal to swing me back here in the morning. I don't care enough to argue. On the drive over to his house, my curiosity builds. I'm more excited than I care to admit that I'm going to get to see Noah's place. Especially since this visit was a spur of the moment one.

When you know company is coming, you have time to clean up and hide your vibrators, or whatever stuff a guy would hide. This is going to be seeing a side of Noah I've never seen before.

I hope he's tidy. He doesn't have to be a neat freak or anything. Still, you can tell a lot about a person by the things they surround themselves with. On second thought, maybe I need his place to be a turn off. Yes, that would be better for my mental health.

When we get to his place he backs his truck and trailer into a garage.

One look around his garage and I'm fairly confident his house won't be messy.

"This is the cleanest garage I've ever seen," I turn in a circle once I'm out of the cab of the truck, looking around.

He smiles. "My tools are my livelihood. I take care of them."

A thrill races up my spine at the thought of being taken care of by a man like Noah Thompson.

CHAPTER 8

Noah

I ALMOST KISSED her earlier, and now she's in my house. Her fingertips coast across the granite of my kitchen island. "Your kitchen is beautiful."

"Thank you." I swallow, liking the vision of her in my space.

"Did you do the work yourself?"

Before I can answer her, she stops me. "You did. I'm sure of it."

"What makes you so sure?" I cock my head to the side in question.

She lifts her shoulder in a gentle shrug. There's drywall dust in her hair and a sleepy expression on her face. "Are you sure you're not gonna pass out in the tub?"

She gives me a sleepy smile. "I've done that before."

My eyes widen. "What?"

She makes a pashaw sound. "Don't worry. I've never drowned."

"You're not making me feel any better," I laugh.

"You can talk to me through the door," she offers. "If I go quiet you can yell at me and wake me up."

I shake my head but know better than to argue her logic. "Right this way."

"I like this room too," she murmurs as we pass through my den. "Is it hard to put wood up on a wall like that?"

"Depends on where you want it."

This question seems to confuse her. "It wouldn't look good everywhere?"

I muffle a laugh with a cough. "How about you sleep on that?"

I lead her down the hall that splits off into the two bedrooms and hesitate at the doorway of mine. My bathroom is the nicer of the two and, if I need to talk to her through the door I'll be more comfortable doing it from my bed.

"It's through here," I say, only slightly disappointed that I'm not showing her my bedroom for another reason.

"Is this your room?" She asks, pausing in the doorway.

"I'm not going to try anything funny," I chuckle, and then explain, "The master bath is nicer than the spare."

"I don't need anything special," she argues.

I disagree. "You haven't seen the bath."

That peaks her interest. She steps into the room and past me, pointing between the door to the bathroom and the master closet in a silent question.

I point to the door on the right and she moves, opening it. I stand back and wait. I don't have to wait long before I hear her gasp.

"Wow!"

"Thanks," I reply.

She spins to face me. "I'm going to take a quick shower first so when I take my bath I'm not soaking in drywall dust."

"Here's your bag. I'm going to shower in the other room," I point with my thumb behind me. "I'll knock on the bathroom door to let you know when I'm back in the room."

"Thanks Noah. For everything."

"You don't have to keep thanking me."

"Try and stop me," she replies, smiling as she closes the door.

The wall of the spare bathroom shares that of the master. While I shower, I try not to think of her wet and naked on the other side of it. My body has other ideas so I turn the water from hot to cold and stand under its stream until I'm able to control my response.

Showered and dressed in a pair of loose pajama pants and an old t-shirt I walk back into my bedroom. I've never stood in here and listened to another person shower.

I've brought women home before but if they showered the next morning, they didn't do it alone. The water turns off and I knock on the door.

"Alright in there?" I ask.

"You have an amazing shower," she calls out in response so I can hear her over the fan.

I grin at my door in agreement.

As I settle myself on my bed, I hear the water turn back on, this time to fill the bath. She surprises me by opening the door.

I sit up, my mouth falling open when she slowly walks into my room, wearing my robe.

"I hope this is okay." Her voice is quiet, with a hint of shyness as she motions to it. "I thought it would be weird if I came out in a towel."

My gaze starts at her bare feet and then travels up her shapely calves. My old terrycloth robe starts there. It covers her but does not hide her figure. I make a point to commit what she looks like, standing in the doorway of my bathroom in my robe, to memory.

"Watching a tub fill is like trying to watch a pot boil," she explains.

Needing to get my mind off of her standing there in my robe, I ask, "You liked the shower?"

Great, now my mind is on her naked in my shower.

She nods. "You're going to regret letting me use it. Now that I know how amazing it is I'm going to pester you to let me use it again, and help me put in one like it at my place."

Settling myself back onto my pillows, I reply, "No pestering needed, and you can use it anytime."

She smiles down at her feet before lifting her face to meet my eyes. "Do you really think we can do something like this at my house?"

"I put this one in. I don't see why we couldn't do it again at your place."

"With the wood stuff on the walls?"

I press my lips together and nod. She turns, and steps back into the bathroom before coming right back out.

"I'm going to get in the tub now." She gestures with her thumbs over her left shoulder.

"Turn off the fan so you don't have to shout," I say as she steps back into the bathroom.

She sticks a hand out, giving me a thumbs up before closing the door and I laugh. I've laughed more in the past few weeks with Finley than I have with any other girl. She's funny, beautiful, and driven. I listen to the sound of water splashing, imagining her stepping into the tub.

"You still awake in there?" I call out.

"Yes," she replies before yawning loudly.

"Don't fall asleep," I order.

"I don't know what I like more, your shower or your tub."

"I'm more of a shower guy."

"Why'd you get the fancy tub?"

"Can't have the tub not hold its own against the shower when it's time for resale," I explain.

"Are you thinking of selling?"

"Not right now, but I don't think I'll live here forever. It was the garage that sold me on it originally."

I hear water splash before she asks. "Do you think I made a mistake not buying a house with a garage?"

Do I tell her I'd never buy a place without a garage, no. "You'll want one when winter comes."

"No, I plan to hibernate in the winter," she argues.

I choke back a laugh. "Hibernate? Like a bear?"

"Sure, you have those up here don't you?" She jokes.

Not touching her bear comment, I ask, "What are you going to do for food?"

"Oh, I'm sure I could pay a delivery service to do it for me."

"What about winter sports? You don't want to go skiing or ice skating?"

She answers my question with one of her own. "Do you have ponds you can skate on out here?"

"Sure. But, most people still go to rinks."

"When I was little I took skating lessons."

"Oh yeah?" I can't help but picture her in one of those sexy skating get ups. "I played hockey."

"You did? Isn't that sport pretty rough?"

"It could be, but we wore pads."

"I'm turning into a prune and I'm having a hard time keeping my eyes open. I'm getting out now."

I listen to the water splash, as she must be stepping from the tub. After a couple of minutes, she comes out wearing flowery shorts and a blue tank. Shifting off my bed, I take her duffle from her.

I cringe when I open the door to the spare room. I forgot about some boxes I had moved in here. Dropping her bag by the door, I grab them off of the bed and shove them into the closet.

"Sorry about that."

She looks around then tilts her head to the side. "You do remember what my house looks like right now?"

I reach up to scratch the back of my head, not wanting to admit I was hoping to impress her.

"If you need anything. Let me know."

"Thank you."

Before I can tell her to stop thanking me, she presses her fingers to my mouth, silencing me. "Let me thank you. Please."

I nod, her fingers moving with my head.

Pulling her hand back she gives me a sweet smile. "Good night Noah."

"Good night Finley."

I close her door behind me but leave my door open in case she needs something during the night. With her across the hall, I expect it to be hard to fall asleep, not taking into account how worn out I am.

Sniffing, I turn my face into my pillow and groan. Most mornings I have no problem waking up. Recently, with the late nights and hard work I've been putting in at Finley's house, mornings have been rough. Sniffing again, my eyes pop open when I smell coffee. That's when my sleep fog lifts and I remember Finley spent the night.

Climbing out of bed I let my nose lead me to her. Her back is to me as I approach.

She not only made coffee, but she's cooking something on the stovetop. "Morning."

With a surprised yelp, she turns, spatula in hand. "You startled me."

I show her my palms. "Sorry about that. It smelled so good I had to come and investigate."

She steps to the side, giving me space to come stand beside her. "I hope you like it."

Mentally cataloging the contents of my fridge I ask, "What is it?"

"I'm calling it a loaded egg scramble," she replies. "There's a little bit of everything in here."

"I didn't have much," I counter.

She turns her face to smile up at me. "Don't forget, I'm an awesome cook so I worked with what I could find."

Impressed, I nod. "Looks good, whatever it is."

I move to pour myself a cup of coffee, pausing to look at hers. "Want more coffee?"

"Yes, please," she replies, pushing the food around with her spatula.

I refill her cup and watch as she slides the egg mixture from the pan onto two plates. I take both our cups and carry them to the other side of my kitchen island where I have stools. She follows me with the plates.

"How'd you sleep?" I ask after we're settled.

Her eyes take on a dreamy look. "Better than I've slept in ages."

She's alone in that. I tossed and turned most of the night thinking about her sleeping in my spare room. The mattress she slept on was mine before I upgraded to a king. "Not too sore?" I press.

She shakes her head. "Between my hot soak last night and the mattress in your spare room, I feel great."

She looked great too.

"Man. This is delicious," I say after taking a bite of her concoction.

"I'm so happy you like it." She takes her own bite and says, 'It does taste pretty good."

"Best breakfast I've had in ages."

She smiles at me. "Get used to it."

I blink. What does she mean by that?

I pat my stomach, deciding not to ruin the mood by asking. "Sounds good to me."

When we're both finished she takes our plates and starts to clean them. "Just leave them in the sink. My cleaning lady comes today. She'll take care of them."

"You have a cleaning lady?"

I shrug. "I like things neat. My parents use the same woman; her name is Lisa. She's got a deadbeat for an ex and kids to take care of."

"That's nice of you." She hesitates by the sink before leaving the plates like I asked.

"What time do you have to start work today?"

Her gaze moves to the clock display on my microwave. "In an hour." She pauses before asking, "Will you have enough time to drop me off before your first appointment?"

I nod. "I'm going to go get ready. You want to take another shower?"

She shakes her head. "All I have to do is change and brush my teeth."

"Wanna race?" I joke.

She blinks and then grins. I take off first. In fairness I should have done a countdown or said go first. That doesn't stop her from grabbing onto the back of my shirt to try and slow me down. We're both out of breath and laughing by the time we reach the end of the hallway.

Quickly stripping, I pull on the first pair of jeans I can find and a polo shirt with our logo on it. Next I pull on a pair of thick wool socks and my work boots. My dentist would lecture me over the amount of time I brushed, so I swish around some mouthwash for good measure. Lastly, I use water from my sink to wet my hair and finger comb. There's no way she's beating me. I congratulate myself before walking out of my room only to find her waiting for me in my den.

She smirks. "What took you so long?"

"How did you beat me?" I ask, dumbfounded.

Her eyes move over my face before settling on my forehead. "Did you do your hair?"

Self-consciously I scratch the back of my head. "All I did was wet it."

She laughs, covering her mouth to muffle it.

"Shut it," I grumble, grinning at her.

She stands, rolling her eyes when I take her bag.

With a full stomach and Fin beside me, I catch myself smiling for no reason more than once on the ride to her house. I could get used to this.

"See you later," I call out my window.

She waves before letting herself in. I stay parked, staring at her front door for a few seconds after it closes behind her.

Then I get my ass in gear since my first appointment is thirty minutes from here, depending on traffic. My schedule for the day is packed, one appointment after another.

Jon meets me at my last appointment for the day since it's for a couple that lives on his street. In theory he could have done this without me. Problem is, people who know us try to use knowing us to get discounts.

If this couple were close friends with either Jon or Emily, maybe we'd cut them a deal. Thing is, this is a business. The materials we use cost money, the equipment we own needs maintenance, and the guys who work for us expect to get paid.

What I'm doing for Finley is on my own time. The material we've used she's paid for. Casual friends don't get that.

My presence, since they don't know me, should keep them from trying to ask for freebies. Jon and I have been doing this long enough to know how to avoid shit like that. What I wasn't expecting was how chatty Jon's neighbors would be. Our meeting goes a full hour longer than it should have.

It would have been rude to step away and text Finley. Because of that, I wait to check my phone until we're finished and I'm in my truck.

There's a text from her asking if I'm okay, and it was sent thirty minutes ago. It unnerves me that I worried her. Instead of texting her, I call her.

"Hey Noah," she answers.

"I'm sorry I'm running late. My last appointment went longer than I thought it would."

"Did they hire you?"

I grin, liking that she was interested. "They did. Contracts signed."

"Congratulations!" she shouts.

It's funny how excited she sounds for something that happens daily.

"How was your day?"

"Are you still coming over? I can tell you when you get here," she replies.

Since I am definitely coming over, I agree and offer to pick up dinner on the way over.

When I pull up, she surprises me by walking out to meet me.

"I think your bathroom has magical healing properties," she greets. "I didn't need to use my hot pad once today."

I laugh, passing her the food bags. "Can I quote you for bathroom remodel advertising?"

She follows me to the back of my trailer and watches as I unload the supplies we'll need to mud and tape what we put up yesterday.

"So, tell me all about your day," I say following her inside.

"Ugh," she groans. "The company I work for changed the system that we use to close out claims. It was supposed to make everything easier only it isn't working right so everything I worked on today took twice as long as it should have."

"That blows."

She nods. "It made today drag on."

"Are they going to fix it?"

"They're working on it but, off topic, I video chatted with my parents today so I could show them all the progress around here."

"That's great."

She smiles, her eyes sparkling with it. "They were so worried when I decided to buy this house. Seeing their faces when they saw everything we've done was really cool." She gulps then adds. "Thank you for that."

I shrug, not bothering to tell her to stop thanking me. "Did you tell them about your new dream bathroom plans?"

Her eyes widen and she shakes her head. "No offense, but no way I'm telling them I spent the night at your house. They'd assume things."

"Oh, right. I didn't think about that."

"They're pretty conservative and with not even being divorced for a year, it wouldn't go over well. Also, I'd hate for them to think badly of you."

I lift my hands. "Don't worry about it. You've only met Abby but once you experience the full Thompson clan you'll get that I understand."

Her posture relaxes. "Your family sounds fun."

"That's one way of putting it."

My family is a curious bunch. It's just a matter of time before they'll force a meeting. I only hope they don't scare her off.

CHAPTER 9

Finley

MY NEW DESK was delivered today, and I just finished putting it together. Since I don't need a living room and a den, I'm using the living room space for it. So, I have an office, or at least a temporary one. Someday, after the renovations to the second floor are done, I plan to renovate the third floor and make it into an office.

It's one giant space with five cool dormer windows. I'll wall off the second half of it for an attic of sorts and the rest of it will be a kick ass office. That's a long ways off though.

I'm going to celebrate this desk since it's the first piece of actual furniture I've bought for my house that's been delivered.

My new sofa should be coming later this week and I can't wait. It was a splurge but since my parents are funding my new kitchen appliances as a Christmas/birthday present, one I could afford. It's a plush, soft, gray sectional, the seats on either end can recline. I ordered it online so I haven't actually sat on it yet but I'm hoping it will be comfortable enough to sleep on. I'm sick of my air mattresses.

Noah told me to just buy an actual mattress already. I will, hopefully after two more paychecks. With his help, this renovation has been going faster than what I budgeted for. When I thought I'd be doing all of this work on my own, I had planned for it to take longer.

Now that Noah is helping me, we're working faster than my paychecks are coming. Also, I had originally planned for a more modest master bathroom. After using Noah's that first time, and at least once a week since, I changed my mind.

The new tub I ordered costs three times as much as the one I was going to get. Don't even get me started on what the multiple showerheads cost. It'll be worth it in the long run.

For now it means that I need to be smarter about my budget going forward. Sure, I bought this house outright so I don't have a mortgage. I have money in the bank but it would be foolish to not leave some of it aside for emergencies.

My major expenses for the remodel are paid for. Furniture, other than what I've already bought, not so much.

"Good looking desk," Noah says from behind me.

I yelp, jumping at least a foot in the air. "Holy crap Noah. You scared me."

He grins mischievously. "The kitchen door was unlocked."

I smack his arm, still trying to catch my breath. "You didn't have to sneak up on me."

His expression softens. "You shouldn't leave your doors unlocked."

"Noted," I grumble, then look back at my new desk. "You like it?"

He comes to stand next to me, folding his arms over his broad chest. "It's a great desk."

I nod, then turn to grin at him. "I love it."

"So, where are we putting it?"

I turn again, spinning to look at the available walls. "What do you think of here?"

His gaze moves to where I point. "It'll work." He moves to one side of my new desk. "Come on. Let's move it."

Apart from the obvious, Noah's reactions to my ideas are night and day different from what I experienced with Allen. No matter what I said, Allen's way was always better. Part of the reason I took this project on was to rebuild my self-confidence. Noah's support has done wonders for more than just this house.

Together, we move my desk to the center of the sidewall, right below a window.

As soon as it's in place we both step back. "Looks good."

I nod in agreement. It does.

"Are you sure you don't want to set it up in the den?" He asks, and then explains, "Your TV is in there."

"I've gotten in a bad habit of having the TV on while I work. This will be better for me."

He does this half smile thing. God, he's so handsome he should come with a warning label. One that says: Will catch you off guard and turn you into a stammering fool if you look directly at him.

There's this boyish quality to him, even though he's all man. It would be a lie to say I'm not attracted to him. I am. Unfortunately, he's done nothing to show me he sees me as anything other than a friend.

He's become so much more than only a friend to me. Since I'd never do anything to risk our friendship, I'm going to need to deal with the fact that's all he'll ever be.

"Let's grab your stuff from the den."

"Okay," I reply, grinning.

The folding table that was serving as my desk is in my den, my TV set up at the end of it. I unplug my laptop and scoop it up, piling its cords, the mouse, and my headphones on top. Noah grabs my notebooks, pens, and a decorative box.

Smiling to myself at what that box contains, I make my way back into my new office. My new desk has a built-in shelf along the back of it, three wide drawers going down each side and one thin drawer across the middle.

I set my laptop down first. My mouse goes to the right of it and my headphones to the left. Then, I feed the cords under the gap below the back shelf.

"Where do you want these?" Noah asks, standing behind me.

"Put them on the shelf for now," I reply, crawling under my desk.

After plugging my laptop in, I back myself out from under my desk on my hands and knees and then sit, my ass to my heels to look at it. He set the box on the center of the shelf. Every time we eat Chinese I swipe his fortune and I've been storing them all in that box.

"You'll need an office chair," Noah suggests.

"I can use the folding chair for now," I shrug.

"Promise to put something under it so you don't scratch up your floors.

I want to grin but I don't, instead I give him a brusque

nod.

He does grin. "Want to go get a rug to put under it?"

He wants to go shopping with me? I know my budget is tight but there's still room in it for things like lamps, rugs, towels and other odds and ends.

"But I thought we were starting the kitchen cabinets today?"

"It's going to take a night, maybe two to assemble them," he replies. "Come on. You know you want to."

Darn the man for being right.

"There was this great rug I saw online. Let me check and see if they have one in stock before we go."

Staying on my knees, I shuffle forward and open my laptop. I'm bad about closing browser windows so it doesn't take long to pull up the one with the rug on it. After a couple clicks, I confirm they have it in stock.

Looking over my right shoulder I point to the screen. "What do you think?"

He closes the distance between us, coming to stand off to my side and leans over me. "I like it."

He steps back, offering me his hand to help me stand. I take it, his long fingers wrapping around mine. His other hand goes to my waist as I stand.

Wetting my lips I whisper, "thanks."

His hand tightens on my waist before he releases me, dropping my hand. "Let's go."

We go out the back way. When I grab my keys and purse, my eyes linger on the boxes that hold my new kitchen cabinets. As if reading my mind, Noah says, "We'll be back in no time."

"Get out of my head," I joke, locking up behind us.

"No trailer?" I ask when I see his truck.

He shrugs. "Didn't need it today. Don't worry, the rug and anything else you pick up will fit in the bed."

When we get to the store, he refuses to let me push the cart.

I stare at him. Every time we've gone somewhere together, he's driven. "Are you one of those guys who always has to drive?"

He frowns but does not deny it.

"What if we're taking my car?" I press.

His brows come together. "Why would we take your car?"

"There's nothing wrong with my car anymore," I argue.

His expression looks like he smelled something bad, making me laugh.

"Well, what if your truck broke down and I came to pick you up?" I ask, not ready to let it go.

"My Chevy would never break down," he scoffs.

I shake my head and tell him to turn left down the next aisle. I'll figure out a way to get him to let me drive. Until then, I'll just appreciate his help. Specifically, the way he hefts the rug and loads it onto the cart.

"Want anything else while we're here?"

I twist my mouth to the side while I think about it. Then I remember all my kitchen cabinets waiting for us.

"Nope, let's go!"

He coughs but it sort of sounds like a chuckle. "I've never met someone so excited to assemble cabinets."

"I'm not weird," I snap. "I'm just so ready to have an actual kitchen again."

"Want me to see if Abby can come over and help?"

Does that mean he doesn't want to be alone with me?

I pause. "Ah, sure."

"She loves assembling stuff," he explains.

"She does? Man, I should have asked her to help me with my desk. That was a bitch to put together," I grumble.

"I'm taking that as a yes," he says, pulling out his phone.

I reach for the handle of the cart but he blocks it stepping in front of me.

"Come on," I cry, and then motion to his phone. "You can't text and push."

Ignoring me, his thumb continues to move over his phone before he hits send and slips it back into his pocket. "All done."

Looking far too pleased with himself, he puts his hands on the handle and starts to push the cart.

"You are such a pain."

He looks over his shoulder at me and winks. My mouth falls open and it takes me a few seconds to move. I meet him at the register. While I pay he pulls his phone back out.

"Abby is in, and she's picking up food," he says as soon as we're out the door.

I grin at him, my earlier annoyance gone. "Let's go."

When we get back to my house he carries my new rug in. Together we unroll it and shift it under my desk. I grab my folding chair from the den to finish the set up.

"You still need a new chair."

I tilt my head to the side and agree, "I still need a new chair."

"Knock, knock!" Abby calls from the kitchen.

"We're in here!" I shout my answer.

When she walks into the room I blink.

Noah on the other hand speaks. "What did you do to your hair?"

She frowns, lifting her hand towards her head. "I got bangs."

"Why?" Noah asks.

I smack his stomach and snap, "Noah."

Abby's face falls. "Do they look that bad?"

I cross the room to her, and take the bag of food from her. "No one said they look bad."

Her fingers start to tug at them. "I thought they looked cute."

Noah makes a noise in his throat and I look over my shoulder to glare at him and mouth *be nice.* Then I turn Abby and usher her back toward the kitchen.

"I like them."

"You do?" Noah asks making Abby groan.

I ignore his terrible question and focus on Abby. "Don't listen to him. What does he know about hair?"

She looks up at me, a hopeful expression on her face. "You really like them?"

I personally have never been a fan of bangs on myself. On her, they *are* cute. I think they'd look better swept to one side but there's no way I'm telling her that now.

"Yes, I do."

"I don't," Noah unhelpfully adds from behind us.

"Shut up!" I snap again.

"No, he's right. I shouldn't have gotten them," Abby moans before running to the bathroom.

I set the bag of food on the nearest pile of boxes before turning on Noah to smack his arm. "Why would you say that?"

He grabs my wrist when I go to smack him again, and then my other wrist when I try with that hand.

Holding my hands between us he says, "I don't lie to my sister."

I tug at my hands but he doesn't let me go. "You could have been nicer about it."

"Why sugarcoat the truth?"

My eyes widen. "What if I got bangs, would you tell me to my face that you didn't like them?"

His gaze stays locked on mine, studying my expression. "No."

"Because you know it would hurt my feelings?" I press.

He nods, letting go of my hands. "And because anything would look good on you."

It would?

His unexpected compliment releases a swarm of butterflies in my middle.

"You need to go talk to her," I stammer and then add, "be nice and tell her you're sorry."

He pulls in a breath before nodding. Moving past me he goes to knock on the bathroom door. While he talks Abby into opening the door, I grab some paper plates and serve up the food Abby brought.

Noah is good, he's got her out of the bathroom and smiling by the time I'm finished. It's fun having Abby join us for dinner. Watching how Noah interacts with her, even after the bangs debacle is sweet.

I didn't have any siblings growing up and envied the kids I knew who did. My cousin Heather and I were close, but it's not the same.

"When are you bringing her to mom and dad's for dinner?" Abby surprises me by asking Noah. "Everyone wants to meet you," she adds to me.

"What? Why?" I sputter, putting down my plate.

We moved a couple of the boxes to form a makeshift table we're sitting around. The bistro table only has two chairs and is so small it wouldn't work for the three of us.

Abby blinks, and then blinks again. "Of course they want to meet you. They're curious about who's taking up all of his time."

"Don't freak her out Abs," Noah says before turning his gaze to me. "You don't have to be nervous about meeting them."

My eyes bug and I look from Noah to Abby and then back to Noah. "*Am* I meeting them?"

He reaches across the table to cover my hand with his. "If you want to. My mom wants to meet you but I didn't want to put you on the spot."

"I—I," I stammer.

"You don't have to," he says, his hand still on mine.

I look over at Abby and she tries to assure me. "But you should. They'll love you."

I gulp. "They'll love me? Why will they love me? They don't even know me."

"How about we talk about it more later. Look at all of these cabinets we need to assemble tonight."

My eyes move to the boxes Noah pointed at. There are a lot of them. Yes, I would prefer to focus on putting my kitchen together. Meeting Noah's parents is freaking me out for some reason.

"Yeah," Abby adds. "We should probably get started on them."

"Okay," I agree, pulling my hand out from under Noah's, I stand.

"I'll clean up here," Abby says. "Start opening those boxes."

"My box cutter is over there."

I see it and get to work.

When the boxes were delivered, Noah and I grouped them by uppers, lowers and corners.

"We should do the base cabinets first," Noah says, coming to stand next to me.

"Why?" I ask, not caring but preferring this subject.

My gaze stays on the box I'm opening but I feel his eyes on me. "We measure the height of where the uppers go off the base cabinets."

"Why not from the ceiling?" I ask as he helps me lift the pieces from the box.

The upper cabinets I ordered go all the way up to the ceiling.

He shrugs, "Since ceilings aren't always level we do it this way."

That has me straightening to look at his face. "Is my ceiling level?"

His ocean blue eyes warm. "Yes, it is."

I quickly look back down at the box. "Just checking."

He softly chuckles beside me but I ignore it. With Abby's help, we unpack each of the base cabinet boxes, careful not to mix them up. Abby starts working on one, not waiting for help from Noah and me.

"Let's work on this one together," Noah suggests, directing me toward the pile closest to us.

I read the first instruction aloud while Noah sifts through the pile to get the pieces we need. Noah wasn't joking when he said Abby likes to assemble things. Even though she's working alone, she starts putting together

her second cabinet before we even finish our first.

When we finish ours, I motion around the room. "Can we set them along the wall so I can see what they'll look like?"

"Of course," Noah replies.

I help him carry both cabinets over to the back wall while Abby keeps working. There's a window overlooking the backyard where my sink will be centered beneath.

I only plan to have cabinets along the back wall and the wall where the oven is to give my kitchen an open feel. The back wall is long enough that I'll have plenty of storage.

I'm not going to put in an island but I might get an old farm table to put in the center of the room for an extra prep area.

"I have cabinets," I grin, looking up at Noah.

"You sure do." He smiles down at me.

For some reason, his smile reminds me that his mother wants to meet me. Has he told her about me? If she wants to meet me that must mean he has. I wonder what he's said. I hope she doesn't think I'm taking advantage of him. Maybe that's why she wants to meet me, to yell at me for using Noah. But, Abby said they'd love me and I'm not using Noah.

"Why are you frowning?" Noah asks, a crease forming between his brows.

I turn away, hoping he doesn't notice my nervousness. By the bunch in his eyebrows, my guess is he knows.

CHAPTER 10

Noah

"**W**HEN AM I going to meet this woman you've been seeing?"

All eyes turn to me. "She's just my friend."

My mom pouts as she shrugs her shoulders. "Friends still need to eat."

"Abby's met her. She'll tell you, Finley can be shy."

Abby lifts her napkin to wipe her mouth before agreeing with me. "She is, Mom. And a bit of a homebody."

My mother ignores both of us. "I want to meet her."

I decide the only way to get her to focus on something else is to change the subject. "Is Asher coming?"

It's my dad who answers. "He didn't say no."

My younger brother tries to come to our family dinners but has a habit of getting caught up in his work and losing track of time.

Everyone else is here, including Brooke and the kids. Whether that means she's moved back in with Eli, I don't know.

"Have you asked her if she'd like to come?" Gideon, being ever helpful brings the conversation back to Finley.

I shift uncomfortably in my seat. "I mentioned Mom wanted to meet her."

"And she didn't want to meet me?" My mom asks, pressing her hand to her chest.

Not the reaction I was expecting.

"No, Mom. It wasn't like that. She got nervous so I dropped it," I explain.

"I don't get what the big deal is," Eli mutters.

"Can we talk about something else?" I plead.

"Yes," Abby replies, then focuses her attention on the kids. "Are you guys ready for school to start?"

In unison, they groan, making the rest of us laugh.

Happy the focus is no longer on me, I watch my mom head to the kitchen and follow her.

"Need any help?" I ask from the door.

She turns, her hands on her hips. "She must be a good influence. You don't normally offer to help me cook."

"Mom," I warn.

She waves me over and motions for me to lean down so she can kiss my cheek. "I'll stop. I only push because I love you."

"I love you too Mom," I murmur, straightening.

Her face softens, and then she puts me to work.

"Are you going to her house after dinner?" Eli asks during a conversation lull at dinner.

"Yes," I reply, leaving it at that.

"What are you going to do when her house is

finished?" He keeps going.

As I glare at him, Abby answers. "They're friends, E."

"Why do you care?" I ask, my eyes on my older brother.

He frowns but doesn't answer me.

"Abby said she's hot," Gideon ventures into the conversation.

Abby, who's sitting to my right huffs, "I said beautiful."

"A woman calls another woman beautiful means a guy would call her hot," Gideon explains.

I can't fault his logic until he adds, "maybe I should swing by her place to see if she needs any landscaping."

He stops laughing at his joke when I catch his eye.

He lifts his hands, his smile still wide. "Still not into sharing your toys, I see."

Abby's lip curls in disgust. "Please tell me you did not just imply women are toys."

He gives her a weak smile. Our sister has no fear, he might be seven inches taller than her but she'll still kick his ass because she fights dirty.

Brandishing her index finger like a sword she points at him. "Take it back and apologize to womankind."

His face remains turned to hers but he chances a side-glance to our mother. Gideon has gotten away with a lot over the years because he was the baby of the family. Insulting women appears to be an exception to this rule when he notices our mom's face.

With an aggravated sigh he grumbles, "I take it back and apologize for saying it in the first place." He then gives Abby his best impression of puppy dog eyes and asks, "Still love me?"

Abby pulls back her hand. "Yes, though I question my sanity for it."

Thankfully, my relationship with Finley doesn't come up again for the rest of dinner. That streak ends not long after when I try to make my goodbyes.

"Hurry back to her like a good little dog," Eli sneers.

I look up at the ceiling in the hopes of finding some patience up there. All I see is my parents' ceiling could use a fresh coat of paint.

I look back down at Eli and ask, "Why is it such a big deal where I spend my time?"

"She's using you and you don't even care," he snaps.

I drag my hand down my face, so sick of not only his assumptions about her but also the fact that he doesn't think I can take care of myself.

"She's not like that," Abby argues before I can.

I rest my hand on her shoulder, giving it a squeeze. "No point trying to talk sense into him. I don't care what he thinks. I'm leaving."

"Noah, don't let some chick lead you around by your dick," Eli grumbles.

He may have meant for only me to hear it but his voice carried with his emotion.

We all turn at Brooke's gasp. Her gaze is on Elijah, a pained expression in them.

"Come on kids," she murmurs, turning to usher the kids out of the room.

"Brooke," Eli, groans, following her.

She doesn't stop though, and when he reaches her she shakes off his hold.

"Why does he have to be such an asshole?"

I shake my head. "Guess it comes natural."

Abby turns to give me a hug. "Sorry bro."

I kiss the top of her head. "You should swing by Finley's place sometime soon. You won't recognize it."

"I might. She texted me some pictures yesterday."

I let her go, shouting a goodbye to our folks. "Pictures don't do it justice. Stop over, okay?"

She nods and promises to come by.

Once I'm in my truck I text Finley to let her know I'm on my way. During my drive, Eli's words replay in my head. I know Finley isn't using me. That doesn't mean I haven't wondered what will happen to our friendship once the work to her house is done.

I've been using her house as the excuse to see her. Once that excuse is gone, where will I be? Granted, the work to her house won't be done anytime soon, and when it is I can always talk her into building a garage.

When I park in front of her place, I sit in my truck for a minute to look at it. The lights are on in both of the front rooms.

She needs curtains or blinds, you can see right in. She's not in either room. If I had to guess, she's in her kitchen. Ever since we put her appliances in, she's been obsessed.

No more takeout dinners for either of us, she's been cooking up a storm. Knowing that, it's sad to see her dining room empty. She should be throwing dinner parties, not just cooking for me.

I climb down from my truck and skip the front door to go knock on her kitchen door.

"Something smells good," I greet when she lets me in.

"I made brownies," she smiles. "How was dinner with the family?"

She's watching me more closely than normal so I ask,

"Did Abby talk to you?"

Her eyes widen before she quickly averts them.

I close the door behind me and lean back against it. "Dinner had its moments."

Her gaze moves back to mine. "Abby called."

I nod. "I figured she would."

"Why does your brother hate me?"

Pushing off of the door I close the distance between us. "He's over protective and going through shit so he needs to put attention on someone else, right now that happens to be me."

"It's my fault for not coming tonight, isn't it?"

I had invited her. When she found out everyone was coming she got nervous so I told her not to worry about it.

"This isn't your fault."

She nods but doesn't look convinced.

"Let me worry about my family."

She frowns then straightens. "I'd like to meet your mom."

I laugh at her expression. "You look like you'd rather have a root canal."

That has her cracking a smile and I decide to change the subject. "You need curtains."

She blinks. "I do?"

I nod. "You can see right into the house."

I bite back a laugh when she ducks and screeches. "Right now?!"

I reach for her hand. "Let's go buy you some curtains. We can hang them up tonight."

Originally, we were going to continue our work

upstairs. So far we've already gutted everything, laid down her new subfloor and put in her new master bath.

While I miss her coming over to use mine, she really wanted to be able to shower in her own home, so we focused on it. We still need to install the drywall and floors for every other room up there.

"I was thinking about getting wooden blinds," she presses her lips together before blowing out a breath like she doesn't want to admit what's about to come out of her mouth. "I read somewhere people who break into houses don't like them."

Even the thought of someone breaking into her house makes my blood boil. I want to tell her I'll never let that happen. "Start with curtains for now and we'll install the blinds after we put in your new windows."

Her head jerks back. "I'm not planning to replace the windows anytime soon."

"You need new ones."

She frowns. "I do not."

"Why do you always have to argue?" I counter.

When she crosses her arms over her chest, all it does is pull my attention to the valley between her breasts. "I'm the boss, remember?"

I drag my gaze up to meet hers. "The insulation we put in your walls is going to help this winter but not by much with the windows you have."

She surprises me by walking out of the kitchen and into her den, where she face plants onto her sectional.

I follow her, sitting near her head and pushing her hair back from her face. "You okay?"

She turns onto her back and looks up at me. "It never ends."

Now is not the time to point out there's a decent

chance she'd only be halfway done with the first floor if I hadn't started helping her.

"Maybe you need a night off from working on the place," I suggest.

She pops up, shaking her head. "No. No, we need to go to the store because people can see in here. Curtains. I've got to get curtains."

I stand and move to her side, offering her my hand. Once she's up, I grasp her biceps.

She gulps, and tips her face up to look at me.

"You're going to get an ulcer if you keep stressing yourself like this."

She nods. "I know. You're right. I know."

My hands glide up and down her arms as she relaxes. It'll piss her off but I decide to cover the cost of her new windows. There's an expression that to get to a man's heart you have to go through his stomach. To get to Finley's heart, I have to go through this house.

She arranged the payment for wood floors going in upstairs around payday. Even if she holds off on the windows for the third floor, she still needs twenty-two windows. That's not counting the French door that leads out to her back patio or the transom and side windows around her front door.

Twenty-two windows will not be cheap, even if I'm doing the labor for free. She could get by with cheap windows but in the long run it'd be more efficient over time to get higher quality ones up front.

"I can get blackout ones," she blurts. "They help on heating bills. Right?"

She doesn't fight it when I take her hand; she just grabs her keys and purse before we walk out the door. After we park, I reach for her hand again and hold it until we get inside. It sucks when I have to let her go to grab a cart.

She's quiet and it's unnerving. Each time I took her hand she didn't flinch. Did she even notice, or was she more preoccupied with the window bomb I dropped?

"Do you like these?" She asks, pulling a display curtain out for me to look at.

I grin at her. "I'm no home decorator."

For the first time since I've seen her tonight she smiles. "You can at least tell me if you think they're hideous or not."

"They are not hideous."

Her nose wrinkles before she huffs, "You're no help."

"You pick out curtains. I'll go get the hardware for them."

She frowns so I say, "or I can stay and help pick out curtains."

She shakes her head and comes over to me, surprising me by hugging me, her arms circling my waist, her cheek pressing to my chest. "I said you were no help but I didn't mean it. I was joking. I'm sorry."

I wrap my arms around her. "Don't worry babe, I knew you were joking."

Her head jerks up in surprise and she stares at me. I hold her gaze, my hands moving up and down, as I rub her back.

She breaks the silence. "Promise?"

I nod. Since she's upset I focus on anything other than how perfect she feels in my arms, her breasts pressed up against me.

She takes a step back. As much as I hate it, I let her go.

"I'm being silly. Go, get the stuff you mentioned and

I'll grab curtains."

"Are you sure?" I ask, taking a step closer to her.

She nods, and goes back to sorting through the curtains on display. "I'm good."

The hardware for the curtains is all in the next aisle. I grab the bare necessities and hurry back to Finley.

"Find anything you like?" I ask her when I make my way back by her side.

She pulls up the first display curtain she showed me. "I like these the best. They're neutral, lined, and even better, on sale. I'm going to use them for the whole first floor." She takes a step to the left and pulls out another curtain. This one has a white background with a pale yellow and grey pattern. "I'm going to put these in the master. I get it's not done yet but since they're the same brand as the others they're on sale too and I like them."

"I like them. Do they have enough of the first curtains for the first floor?"

She moves closer to me, and counts. "Crap. They don't. It's only enough for the living room and dining room."

She pulls out her phone and starts tapping away with her thumbs. "Let me check online."

After a minute she holds her phone up in victory. "Ordered online for pick up later this week."

I load what they do have into the cart as she gets enough curtains for her bedroom and then some sheers.

"I feel good about this," she says as we make our way to the registers.

I'm not sure if her words were for herself or me. "Your house is looking more like a home everyday."

"More like a home," she repeats, a soft smile on her face.

When she sees the total at the register, she gulps before paying. I want to offer to cover it for her but I already know she'd never let me. It'll be hard enough doing the windows for her.

"Are you okay?" I ask, once we're driving back to her house.

She gives me a tight smile. "I was doing math in my head."

"How's your budget looking?" I ask.

"Well, the materials we need for the next couple of weeks are already paid for. The idea of buying windows this soon wasn't something I had considered. It threw me off. But, now that I've had some time to let it sink in, I understand your point in needing to replace them."

"I didn't mean to do that," I admit.

She reaches across the console to squeeze my arm. "I appreciate it. It's better to know and be able to plan for it instead of having to scramble on the fly."

"Scrambling is bad unless it's eggs," I joke.

She doesn't laugh. "How much do you think windows will cost?"

"I'd have to measure your windows to make sure we wouldn't need to special order them. Otherwise, decent ones can range from three to six hundred dollars."

"Six hundred dollars?" She pants.

"Babe, calm down," I order, kicking myself for telling her the truth.

"No, I'm calm. I am," she nods her head, like she's convincing herself.

I don't believe her.

She's quiet the rest of the drive and as we unload her purchases. As soon as we have everything inside, she pulls out a calculator. When I take it from her and shove it into my back pocket she scowls up at me.

"Not now Finley. We have curtains to hang and you promised me a brownie."

Her scowl disappears as she tries not to smile. "The brownies were for something else I made."

My brows furrow. "Do I get to try what you made?"

She smiles outright this time, her attention off of the windows, before dashing off to the kitchen. While I wait, I get started on the first window.

I'm not far along before Finley shouts for me to go to the den. I do as I'm told and watch as she approaches, carrying two glass dishes. Whatever dessert is in them appears to be stacked.

"What are these?" I ask, accepting one from her.

There's a spoon already in it.

"It's a chocolate mousse trifle," she replies, and then points out each layer. "Brownie, mousse, whipped cream, another layer of brownies, mousse, more whipped cream and shaved milk chocolate on top."

"Jesus, it's almost too pretty to eat." When her eyes widen I add, "I said almost."

Then I take a bite and groan, my eyes rolling back. She giggles, clearly loving my reaction before taking her own bite.

Not even caring that I'm not done chewing I mumble, "This is amazing."

She takes another bite, licking her lips after. What I would give to lick this chocolate mousse stuff off her.

"I'm not going to be able to get off of this couch. I'm going to be in a chocolate coma after this," she jokes.

I don't share my reason for not being able to stand.

CHAPTER 11

Finley

"**W**HEN CAN WE come out and see all the work you've done?" My mom asks.

"Come now," I laugh.

"Honey, are you pulling my leg or are you serious? Because if you are serious I'll pop on to the computer and book the next flight."

My chest tightens. I've missed them so much. The moment I got my new mattress and box spring I knew it was finally time for them to come out. They can sleep on my new bed while I sleep on the sofa or my stacked air mattresses.

"Book it," I whisper, my throat thick with emotion.

"Well shit. If you cry, I'm going to cry," she whispers back.

My laugh is wobbly when I choke out, "You cussed."

"It happens," she laughs back. I can just picture her shrugging her shoulders and smiling.

There's a knock at my door and my eyes move to the

131

time display on my microwave. "Crap mom. We've been on the phone for an hour and Noah is here. I gotta go."

"Will we get to meet him when we come out?"

I hurry to open the door. "Of course mama."

Once my door is open I point to my phone and motion for Noah to come in.

"I can't wait to meet him!" she shrieks.

I blush, hoping my parents don't get the wrong idea about our friendship. As much as my feelings for Noah have grown, he only sees me as a friend and I need to be okay with that.

"Alright, Mama. I love you."

"I love you too, honey. Big hugs and kisses from your dad and me until we can get there and hug you for real."

"Okay, email me once you book something."

"I will. Bye honey."

I look up to lock eyes with Noah. "Bye."

"How's your mom?" He asks once I hang up.

"She and my dad are going to come out for a visit to see the house," I explain, my face hurting from my grin.

"That's great news," he smiles.

It hits me how awful I would be to ask him to meet my parents since I've avoided meeting his family, minus Abby, who doesn't count since I met her first.

"Do your parents still want to meet me?" I blurt.

He blinks, doesn't do anything for a couple of seconds and then nods.

I had a couple of logical, I thought at the time, reasons for being scared about meeting them. I didn't want to read too much into our friendship. When he first mentioned it, I had flashbacks to meeting Allen's parents for the first time. It did not go well.

"Are they busy tonight?"

He cocks his head to the side and gives me a lopsided grin. "You want to meet my folks?"

I nod, my stomach flipping.

He keeps his eyes trained on me as he pulls his phone from his pocket. "Hey Dad. Got any dinner plans?"

I try not to hyperventilate as I listen to him agree that we will meet his parents at some restaurant I've never heard of. Before he's done talking I start heading for the stairs.

"Where are you going?" He calls out after me.

"I can't wear this!" I shout. "I need to change."

"What you're wearing is fine," he argues.

I skid to a stop. "Are you joking?"

His eyebrows go up an inch but he doesn't respond. I roll my eyes and get moving. What I'm wearing is fine? That man has lost his mind. There's no way on earth I can meet his parents wearing ratty old sweat pants and a tank top.

I need to change. Since we hadn't started working yet I'm not sweaty. I tug on a comfortable cotton dress with three quarter sleeves. It's not that fancy but it won't wrinkle and I can dress it up a bit with a cute cardigan and ballet flats.

As soon as I'm dressed, I dash into my gorgeous bathroom to fix my hair and swipe on some mascara. It's the best I can do on short notice.

Noah's back is to me when I walk into the den. "All set."

He turns at my words and stops dead. His gaze drops to my feet and then moves upward. When his eyes reach my face, he wets his lips. Holy crap. The last thing I need is for him to draw attention to his lips, his full sensual lips.

"You look—"

When he doesn't finish his sentence I start to worry. Maybe what I think is cute he thinks is hideous. I had assumed he liked what I was wearing but that could be the face he makes when he's disgusted by clothing.

"I look what?" I ask.

"Beautiful," he rasps.

I gulp.

Okay, apparently he was not disgusted.

"Thank you," I whisper and then add, "I'm nervous."

He grabs my hand. "You have nothing to be nervous about."

It's not until he leads me to the passenger side of his truck that I realize he's held my hand the entire way. Okay, he's called me babe and held my hand other times, too, but hasn't tried to make a move. Or is this a move?

My knees bounce as we drive. "Have you eaten here before?"

He grunts his assent. "Best frappes in Woodlake. I've been there a hundred times."

"What's a frappe?" I ask.

"Like a milkshake but better."

"Sign me up," I giggle.

When we park he points out his dad's SUV. "They're here."

Suddenly nervous, I start to wring my hands together. "Maybe this isn't a good idea," I murmur.

His response is nonverbal. He steps down from his truck, walks straight to my side, opens my door, and leans over me to unhook my belt before helping me down. Once my feet hit the ground his hand reclaims mine, giving it a squeeze.

The hostess grips the edge of her podium when she sees us. "Hi Noah."

He lifts his chin in acknowledgement, and asks, "Hey Mindy. We're meeting my folks."

She turns, pointing with her breasts as much as she does with her hand. "Want me to walk you back?"

He doesn't seem to notice but I do. Her body language towards Noah shouldn't make me jealous but it does. I mean, I'm standing right here holding his hand.

He shakes his head. "No, thanks. We can manage."

He leads me, his hand still wrapped tight around mine. I don't know if he's holding it to keep me from running. Why am I so nervous?

When he stops us at a table, I can see the family resemblance at once. Noah gets his build from his father and his coloring from his mother.

They both stand, Mr. Thompson offering me his hand and Mrs. Thompson coming to kiss my cheek.

"Hello." Even I can hear the nerves in my voice. I swallow, the back of my neck beading with perspiration.

Mrs. Thompson's eyes lock on our joined hands. With a gentle tug, I pull it free. He smoothly moves to pull out my chair.

"Finley, these are my parents, Daisy and Dennis.

Mom, Dad, this is Finley."

"It's so nice to finally meet you, Mr. and Mrs. Thompson."

"Please, no Mr. And Mrs. Thompson. You can call me Daisy and him Dennis or Denny," Daisy says as she sits.

"I'm sorry I wasn't able to come to dinner before—"

My excuse is cut off with a wave of her hand. "Don't

you worry about that."

Some of my tension melts away. I'd built up meeting his family into this thing to be afraid of. Two minutes with them proved how wrong I was.

"Noah says you do customer service from your house for a travel company. Do they send you any fun places as a perk?" His dad asks once we're settled.

I shake my head and smile warmly at him. "It'd be cool if they did, but sadly, no."

"I've been trying to talk Dennis here into taking me on a cruise," his mom complains.

His dad frowns at her. "I told you I'd go."

Mrs. Thompson glares at him. "To Alaska? You told me to book a cruise to Alaska. I've seen enough snow and ice to last me a lifetime. I want to go somewhere tropical."

His dad grumbles something about climates and sunstrokes as our server takes our drink orders.

I go for a chocolate frappe. Noah grins at me as I order it. My attention is pulled away from him when Mr. Thompson grunts. Mrs. Thompson is all smiles as she tucks her elbow to her side.

Did she just elbow him?

"I'll take a chocolate frappe too," Noah orders.

This time I don't miss his mom elbow her husband.

"I see. I see," he groans. "Stop poking me."

"Shhh," she whispers.

Noah presses his lips together and folds his arms across his chest.

"I'm only happy to see you looking so happy. It's all a mother could hope for."

Oh boy. Do they think we're dating?

"Mom," Noah warns.

She bugs her eyes at him.

"Oh leave your mom alone. It's her job to pester you kids."

They think we're a couple. My eyes flash to Noah, who is cool as a cucumber next to me. Did he tell them we're together?

With each minute that passes where Noah doesn't set them straight, my anxiety grows. "Noah's been explaining and showing us pictures of all the work you two have been doing on your house," Mrs. Thompson boasts. "We'd love to see it in person sometime."

"Mom," Noah laughs. "You can't just invite yourself like that."

She purses her lips. "I don't see what the big deal is."

"Of course you can come by," I blurt, not wanting them to argue. Then without thinking better of it, I make it even worse. "My parents will be visiting soon. Maybe you could both come over for dinner."

She elbows Mr. Thompson again. "We'd love to."

Noah stretches his arm out to rest across the back of my chair.

"Abby said you were pretty and she was not lying."

Oh wow. "Thank you."

Noah's hand squeezes my shoulder.

As wonderful as that feels, this is bad. If his parents think we're together, do his brothers think the same thing? It's one thing for him to be helping me with my house out of friendship, but another entirely as a girlfriend.

God, I don't even want to know how they think I'm repaying him if that's the case. If that wasn't bad enough, I had to go ahead and suggest a family dinner with my parents. What was I thinking? It will only perpetuate their assumption we're in some sort of a relationship and I don't even have a table for anyone to sit at during dinner.

My mom has been fishing for details about Noah every time we talk. Once she sees him in person she'll have her heart set on him for me. The problem with that is I'm not ready for a relationship. Hell, I'm not sure I'll ever be ready for a relationship. His parents are going to be upset when they learn we aren't really a couple.

Noah and I need to talk but there's no way we can now. For now, I smile, and answer his parents' questions, and drink my frappe.

When the bill comes, Noah pays, shaking his head when I reach for my purse.

Noah and his damn need to pay for food. It dawns on me, he's paid for every dinner I haven't made myself. I stare at him.

'What?' he mouths.

My head is spinning too much to reply. When the server returns with the credit slip for him to sign, we all stand.

Noah reclaims my hand and his parents follow us out to the parking lot.

"It's a good thing you two didn't get into a car accident. Dealing with insurance companies wouldn't be a healthy way to start a relationship," Mrs. Thompson jokes, pulling me into a hug.

My eyes widen and it's an effort not to gasp at her words. I had no idea Noah told her about the day we met, or that we were in a relationship. When she releases me, Mr. Thompson reaches out and gives my arm a squeeze. His movement reminding me of my dad. He's not a hugger either.

Noah and I stand side by side and wave once their SUV pulls away. As soon as they turn onto the road I turn on Noah.

"They think we're a couple."

He shrugs.

My mouth drops open, panic setting in. "Why do your parent's think we're together?"

With his hand on the small of my back, he guides me to his truck. "Abby knows we're not dating."

He opens my door. What he doesn't do is reply.

I climb in and stare as he rounds the hood to get in on his side. "Why aren't you answering me?"

He shrugs, AGAIN, and pulls on his belt. "Noah. We can't let them think we're together."

"Why not?" He breaks his silence by asking.

"Why not?" I repeat his words only louder and somewhat shrilly.

"What's so bad about people thinking we're dating?"

My mouth falls open. "It's not the truth for one."

He turns his head, his eyes laser focused on mine, the intensity in them bringing the temperature of the cab up at least ten degrees. "There's an easy fix for that."

"Yes," I agree. "You should call them and set them straight."

When he doesn't say anything I lift my chin and add, "Right now."

He swallows, his Adam's apple shifting. "I had a different idea."

And then, Noah Thompson kisses me.

Kiss isn't the right word. Well, technically it is but it isn't. To describe it as only a kiss would be saying it was like any other kiss I've ever been given before. It was not.

The mechanics and required parts were all there, his lips, my lips, touching. It was most definitely a kiss, but at the same time it was absolutely not.

Could it be the way his fingers threaded into my hair? Or the warm soft fullness of his lips pressed to mine?

My heart racketed about like a pinball in my chest. Heat blossomed from my gut upward, creeping toward my neck. His lips part and he nips at my bottom lip before pressing firmly to mine again.

This moment, this sweet lip press that didn't even involve tongues affected me more than any experience during my ten-year marriage.

It's that thought that has me pull away, turning my face.

"Finley," he calls.

I shake my head. "I want to go home."

"Come on. Talk to me," he begs.

I shake my head again, looking anywhere but at him. "Please take me home."

Where only seconds ago the temperature in his truck was skyrocketing, it now plummets. The ride to my house is packed with uncomfortable silence broken more than once each time he pleads for me to talk to him.

I'm too upset and confused to do so. Each time he asks, I shake my head. He's my friend. I'm not ready to wrap my brain around him being anything other than that right this second.

It's one thing to be attracted to him. I had that under control. It's better this way, if we're friends no one will get hurt. We can keep working together and when my house is done, we can find another project. He said something about extending the deck off the back of his house.

Or we could do other things. I could cook for him and he can help me explore more of Woodlake. I haven't ventured outside of the immediate area around my place. His parents seemed nice too. It'd be nice to see them again once he makes sure they know we aren't dating.

Other than my neighbors, the only friends I've made here are Noah and Abby. I don't want things to get weird with either of them. But after that more than a kiss, that ship might have sailed with Noah.

Why did he have to do that?

When he parks in front of my house I jump out. His footfalls echo behind me. He overtakes me at the front door.

"We have to talk about this."

I glare at his boots. "I'd like some time to gather my thoughts first."

Gentle fingers, pads rough from work, tip my chin up to look at him. "You're pushing me away."

Lines mar his forehead, a frown etched across his jawline.

"I can't lose your friendship," I whisper. All at once his face softens, the hardness vanishing.

"Do you know what my dad always calls my mom?"

He knows I don't.

His thumb brushes across my jaw. "Best thing he ever did was marry his best friend."

Does he think I'm his best friend and that we should get married?

My nose starts to sting and my lips part. "Am I your best friend?"

It's silly to apply a term that evokes images of preteen girls and friendship bracelets to our relationship. What

141

he's come to mean to me transcends that.

I was in way over my head when I moved here. If he hadn't of swooped in I would have drowned without him. I thought fixing this place up would fix me. Without his help, this project would have broken me at my core.

What Allen did to me shook my confidence and made me question my ability to trust again. I had a plan, a stupid sad plan to protect my heart by moving across the country to live in a place where no one knew me.

I wasn't going to make friends. If I didn't make friends there'd be no risk of getting attached to anyone. He ruined everything.

The right side of his mouth hitches up. "Yes."

His thumb continues to move on my jaw, heat pools in my belly.

"No, I'm not," I argue. "Jon is."

He shakes his head, that smile of his widening. "I don't spend every night with him or miss him every time I leave him."

"Noah," I murmur.

"Shhh," he replies, his thumb moving away from my chin to slide across my bottom lip.

I gulp and stare up at him.

His gaze is locked on his thumb as it moves across my lip again.

"I wanted to kiss you the first time I saw you," he admits.

"Here?" I breathe.

He shakes his head and moves closer to me. "You almost crashed into me."

"That's crazy."

His thumb leaves my lip but stays warm on my skin

as his face dips close to mine. "Only crazy thing is that I waited this long."

I open my mouth to question his sanity. I was sick; I was exhausted, how could he possibly want to kiss me.

I'm cut off from saying anything when his mouth crashes into mine.

CHAPTER 12

Noah

AFTER FINALLY KISSING her, leaving Finley last night was one of the hardest things I've ever done. I wanted to take her home and to my bed. As much as I want her, I would have been happy just sleeping beside her. The only reason I did leave her was because she said we could talk this morning.

I park in front of her house, a place that feels more like home at this point than my own. By the time I make it to the front door, she's opening it.

"Good morning," I murmur, wanting to kiss her again but wanting her to slam the door in my face even less.

"Hey. Come on in," she replies, her tone uncertain.

Each time I enter her home the magnitude of the changes we've made strikes me. The bulk of the renovation to her first floor is complete. It's taken three months of working almost every night and on the weekends. All that's left is to finish furnishing and decorating.

Upstairs, the walls are up and primed, plus the floors

are down. We need to do some more painting and install her hall bath.

We've done so much, part of me is scared she doesn't need me anymore. She can paint on her own and leave the hall bath until she can hire someone or, after helping on the master, try to tackle it on her own.

If she doesn't kick me out it's because she wants more than my ability to swing a hammer.

"I made some muffins," Finley offers, gesturing toward her kitchen.

With a nod, I catalog her stance, her expression and her tone. I'm on edge waiting to see what she'll say, but she's cool as a cucumber.

She twists, her movements smooth as she walks away from me. I follow her.

"About last night," I start.

She looks over her shoulder at me, her hazel eyes weary and shakes her head. "I need more coffee first."

Her putting off our conversation for coffee is both infuriating and endearing. This isn't the first Saturday morning I've been over here this early. Her coffee first demand isn't new.

"Of course."

We move together well in her kitchen, reminding me that this isn't our first dance. I'm hyperaware of her body in relation to mine. Her dark chocolate locks are pulled up in a ponytail and she wears loose track pants and a snug tank.

The material of the straps on the back of her shirt coming up in a t-shape, and the thick straps of an exercise bra visible on either side of it. There's something about the small vision of creamy skin exposed between each strap that makes me unable to look away.

My eyes glide over her skin in ways I wish my hands could.

Her hands hug her coffee mug as she walks into her den. I follow with a mug of my own and a plate of muffins. When she sits I pause. Her couch is a sectional and could easily seat seven adults. Do I sit next to her or give her space?

Patting the cushion to her right, she answers my unspoken question. Stacked milk crates wrapped with a bungee cord serve as her coffee table. Sitting where she motioned, I lean forward to set my mug and plate down.

As good as her cooking is, I can't eat until I know what she's thinking.

"About last night," I start again.

She lifts her hand, stopping me. "I need to say something first."

Swallowing, I nod.

"You know I'm divorced."

"That isn't an issue."

She shakes her head. "That's not what I'm trying to say. Please listen."

I inhale but don't speak.

"My divorce was finalized only months ago. I'm a mess. My decision-making skills at the moment are terrible. Look at this place."

I look from right to left when she glares at me for not looking.

"I bought this house. If you hadn't talked me into letting you help, I would still be sleeping on two air mattresses in my office. And, it's starting to get colder outside. You cleaned my chimneys and found that bird nest saving me from dying in a future house fire."

Future house fire?

Oh shit, she's having a *what if* spiral. Abby is famous for them.

"No what if's. If you want to argue you can't make good decisions I'll argue you made a helluva good one the day you agreed to take my help."

A frown line forms across her forehead.

"You also made a very good decision wearing that dress last night," I blurt.

Her frown line deepens when her eyebrows shoot up. I reach for her mug, taking it from her. Turning away from her, I set her mug next to mine on the milk crate.

Her eyes are on it when I turn back to face her.

"And, another one when you let me kiss you."

She only looks at me when I take her hands in mine.

"You can't look me in the eyes and tell me you didn't feel anything last night."

Her gaze shifts from my face to our joined hands. "It's too soon."

"That's your fear speaking," I argue.

She looks up, her eyes glassy.

"It is," she agrees.

I want to kick myself. Using my hold on her hands, I pull her closer before wrapping my arms around her. She tucks her face into my neck. I rest my cheek on the top her head.

"I'm not going to hurt you," I whisper into her hair.

"There's no way to avoid it," she whispers back.

I pull away slightly. "What does that mean?"

She gulps. "My parents have been together for forty years and I was married for ten. When you let someone in, two things happen. Their hurt becomes yours as well and if one day they decide they don't want you anymore, they leave. When they leave, it isn't a surprise for them. They've been doing it without you knowing it for months. They've already started seeing someone else. When they leave, it's just another day, but for you it's a shock."

"Finley—"

"I had a plan. It was a bad plan but it was all mine. My friends and family were going to stay in Texas and I was going to be here all by myself."

"Why are you so sure you should be alone?"

"It's safer that way."

"You're not built that way." I ease her even closer. "You're trying to punish yourself for picking the wrong man."

She pulls back and I lift my head, watching as she tips her chin up until her eyes lock on mine. "You don't know someone is wrong until it's too late."

"I'm not wrong."

"I need you to be my friend," she whispers.

"Nothing more?" I ask.

She nods and I fight back my impulse to throw her over my shoulder like some caveman.

"Forever?" I push.

She nods again. My chest tightens as my fingers itch to pull out my hair. Knowing she's only trying to protect her heart is what stops me from losing it.

Still, not wanting to let this farce go on anymore, I shake my head. "Nope."

Her lips part and I can't take my eyes off them.

"You're wrong about this and I'm going to prove it to you."

"Noah—"

"No, listen to me. I'm not going anywhere."

I press my lips to hers and am encouraged when she doesn't pull away.

It's not a long kiss. I don't want her to push me away. For now, we're going to be friends that kiss. As soon as she settles into that, we'll be friends that do more than kiss.

Much more.

"I'm not sure I can do this."

"It's okay," I reply. "I'm sure enough for the both of us."

I reach around her to reclaim her mug and then pass it back to her. Then I keep her close tucked to my side.

"Is this okay?"

She's skittish at first but tentatively lifts her mug to her lips for a sip. With each second that passes, her body relaxes against mine.

She never answered my question so I ask differently. "This so bad?"

"It's—" she hesitates before saying, "not."

I grin. I can work with this. After she takes another drink, I shift both of us to grab my plate.

"I know you're freaked." She stiffens and I keep going, "I'm not going to push it anymore now, but this conversation isn't over."

She gulps but doesn't pull away.

"Did you hear back from your mom?"

My question gets her moving, out of my arms and off of the couch. "I was so distracted I forgot to tell you. They're coming today."

I forego my muffins and coffee. "Are they flying into

Manchester?"

She nods and I stand. "When does their flight land?"

"Five o'clock."

"Alright. Is there anything around here you want done before they get here?"

She nods again and I bite back a laugh. "We're tight, babe, but I can't read your mind."

Her face softens, a smile peeking from the corners of her mouth. "Can we paint upstairs?"

I grab my coffee and down it. "You cut the edges, and I'll roll."

All tension from earlier is gone. We've worked together long enough it's easy to ease back into the routine of it.

"What are your parents like?"

When she doesn't answer, I set my roller back in the tray and turn to look at her. "Finley?"

She's on a stepladder, paintbrush suspended in midair. "They're best friends."

Just like my parents.

She rests her brush on her paint filled cup and climbs down the ladder. "I'm going to open the windows in the other room to help with fumes."

She's running away. I get back to painting and let her come to terms with the epiphany she just stumbled upon. She's trying to protect herself. As soon as she figures out I'm on her side she'll get that she doesn't need any protecting from me.

"Okay, all better," she chirps, coming back in.

It doesn't take long to get one coat of paint on the walls. There's no furniture to move and the floors were already covered.

"How do you stay so clean when you paint?" She asks, breaking the silence that had ensued since she came back.

Frowning, I look down at my clothes and then at her. My frown shifts into a smile.

"How do you get so much paint on yourself?" I counter.

Shocking the hell out of me, she jabs me in the chest with her paintbrush. My chin dips as I look down at the glob of off-white paint now marring my maroon tee.

Lifting my roller I grin. "You're going to regret that."

With a squeak she turns toward the door. Lunging, I hook her by the waist and haul her flush against me.

"Noah," she exhales.

"Shh. I'm looking for a clean spot."

Squirming in my hold she lifts her paintbrush.

"Don't even think about it," I warn.

Ignoring me, she drags her brush across my forearm.

Dropping my roller into the pan, I pluck her brush right out of her hand.

"No," she shouts, reaching for it.

I hold it up above our heads as she turns to face me. Pushing up onto her toes she tries to get it back from me. Her hand is on my shoulder, her breasts pressed to my chest. She has no idea what her physical proximity does to me. All I want to do is kiss her, instead I brush some paint onto her cheek.

"Noah," she snaps, stepping away.

"What?" I innocently ask.

With a huff she spins and leaves the room muttering something about washing her face as she goes.

My gaze follows her and I will my body back under

my control. It's a full minute before I start to clean up all of the paint. She hasn't decided what colors she wants to use so we've been using standard builders' beige.

After I clean and pack up all of the materials into one of the spare bedroom closets, I head downstairs. Finley can cook and bake like a master, but that doesn't mean I can't make a damn good sandwich.

I don't turn when I hear her footsteps behind me. "Want one?"

"Yes, please." There's a touch of a Texan twang to her voice. I'm not sure what it is but I can't stop thinking about her someday saying please when I have her in my bed.

Snapping my attention to the food in front of me, I will the hardening in my boxers to stop. She chatters away behind me but I can't hear a word of it until I have my body back under my control.

She pulls a pitcher of sweet tea from her fridge. Before her, I drank mine unsweetened. She's converted me since then.

"I want a table."

That statement has me turning my head to look at her. "Okay. There are a few places around here that sell tables and chairs. Want to check them out after we eat?"

"Can we build one?"

I choke back my surprise. "Sure, but not before your parents get here."

She walks out of the kitchen and before I can stop her and agree to build her a table right now, she comes back holding her cellphone. "What about something like this?"

On her phone is a how-to video of a man attaching legs to a paneled door. The process to attach all four legs takes the man twenty minutes from start to finish. We sell legs like the ones he uses at Thompson's for five to ten bucks a pop, depending on how tall of a leg you get. Finley and I found an old door in her shed weeks ago.

"You sand the door and I'll go get the legs." I tell her, my own excitement building.

Still holding her phone, I catch her when she throws her arms around my neck to hug me. Closing my arms around her, I let her warmth seep into me.

"Thank you," she murmurs.

Not wanting to, slowly, I let her go and set her phone on the counter. "I'll set up the sawhorses and grab the door from the shed."

She surprises me again, this time by framing my face with her hands and kissing me.

She's gone before I can react. I watch her go, my eyes entranced by the way she moves. Yep, I can work with this. Once she's out of sight, I pick up my sandwich and eat it as I walk out to her shed. The door she was talking about is on top of a pile of junk. Finishing my last bite, I hold onto part of the frame and stretch to reach the door.

Pulling it out of the shed, I inspect it for wood rot. Pleased to find it in good shape, I carry it to the back of the house and lean it near her kitchen door.

"I've got a sawhorse," Finley says, trying to carry it and hold open the kitchen door at the same time.

"Here, let me," I say, hurrying over to take it from her.

"I'll get the other one," She replies as soon as I have it.

This time I meet her in the kitchen and she holds the door for me. While I set up the sawhorses and place the door on them, Finley gets my sander.

"Want me to pick up some wood stain?" I ask.

She shakes her head. "I can run out with my dad tomorrow. He'll get a kick out of helping me with this."

"I'll be back," I reply and lean in to press my lips to her temple.

Kissing her last night unlocked this need to touch her, kiss her. I can't keep my hands off of her.

"Surprised to see you in here today," Eli says when I walk up to the register with what I'll need to turn her door into a table.

"Surprised to see you up front."

He frowns. "I had to fire Vicky today."

"No way. That sucks," I say, trying to remember which one Vicky was.

There're some employees at the hardware store who have been here since I was in high school. Then there're short timers who don't stay long at all.

"What'd you have to fire her for?" I ask.

"She was always late. Since it was never more than five minutes I let it go but." He points up to a camera aimed at the register. "I caught her on the tape pocketing a fiver from the till."

I shake my head. "What's wrong with people?"

He nods. "Fucking sucks. I've been going over all of the tapes to make sure I didn't miss her taking more and until I can hire her replacement, I need to cover for her."

"Want me to see if Justin can come help out? You'll have to pay him but he knows his way around the store and can work in the afternoon."

Eli blinks. "Thanks."

I punch his arm. "Don't sound so surprised."

Finally, we had an entire conversation where he didn't give me shit about Fin. As much as we can get on each other's nerves, he's still my brother. I load up my truck and head back to Finley's.

She's still sanding when I get back.

Since she won't hear me over the noise of the sander, I reach over and unplug it.

"Hey!" she complains when it stops working.

"Hey yourself," I greet, and then peer over her shoulder. "How does it look?"

She twists her face to look back at me. "I love it."

I shift away from her and drag my fingers across the wood. The sanding smoothed away layers of black paint, leaving a cool distressed pattern.

"That's good news because I bought something I think you'll like." I tell her, not being able to keep the smile off my face.

She squints at me. "You got me something?"

"Wait here," I order.

At the store they sell sheets of acrylic that can be cut to size. The door Fin wants to use is paneled. She can cover it with this clear sheet to make it a level dining surface.

I set it on the door, and start to unroll it.

Once she sees what I'm doing, Finley jumps to help. "This is perfect."

"We'll need to mount it so it won't move while you're using it."

"It's—" She pauses, looking from her table and then to me. "Amazing. Thank you."

"Anytime. It felt pretty smooth. Were you done sanding?"

She grins. "Just about, it's beat up at the bottom of the door. I was finishing up on it."

I roll the acrylic back up. "You finish up that part and

I'll get the legs ready."

I drill a hole into the center of each leg and then screw a hanger bolt into each one.

"Can we flip the door now?" I ask, as soon as I'm done.

She nods, unplugging the sander and then moves to one end.

After we flip it on the sawhorses, she asks, "Can I do the drilling?"

Can she do the drilling? If she weren't at the other end of that door, I'd kiss her right now. Picking up my drill and one of the metal leg plates, I move to her. Before I give her either, I press my lips to hers. Her hands move to grip my waist. She doesn't pull away and I'm grateful for it.

"Of course you can," I rasp, after breaking our kiss.

I hold the plate steady for her while she drills in each wood screw. As soon as we have all four plates mounted, we screw each leg in.

"Ready to flip it over and see how it looks?" I ask.

She nods excitedly.

Once it's flipped, her eyes go dreamy. It's the same look she gets whenever what we're working on starts taking shape.

We'll need to clean off the dust from sanding before we mount the clear top, and the legs are unfinished so Finley and her dad will still have a project they can work on together.

"I'll get some cleanser and a rag."

When I reach the kitchen door, I glance back at her and find her watching me. She bites her lip but doesn't look away.

I don't care how long it takes, I will earn her trust.

And then her heart.

CHAPTER 13

Finley

I THINK I agreed to date Noah. My gaze drifts to him and then over to my father sitting in the front passenger seat.

"He's so handsome," my mom whispers from beside me.

After Noah and I finished my new table, we went to a store to buy chairs. I almost passed out when I saw how much they were, so Noah took me to a second hand shop instead. I wasn't able to find enough matching chairs that I liked to make a complete set.

It worked out though because I found two cool benches that I'm going to use with two of the chairs. I got all four for less than one chair from the other place. We brought them back to my house and set up my dining room. I was so overwhelmed by how great it looked I agreed to let Noah drive me to the airport.

Why is it impossible to say no to him?

My plan has now morphed into a new plan, one that includes Noah. After all of our kisses, I've decided I want to keep on kissing him. I've also decided, after experiencing his body pressed to mine, I don't want that to end either.

I've worked side by side with him for months now. I feel like I know him better than my ex-husband of ten years. That doesn't mean I'm anywhere near ready to dive into this. No, I'm sitting on the edge of the dating pool with my toes in. But so far, the water feels great.

"I know," I whisper back.

"Why didn't you tell me you started seeing each other?" She asks, her voice low so it won't carry to the front row.

"It only happened last night," I admit.

Her eyes widen and move back to Noah. "I can't wait to tell Charlotte and Jane."

My aunts are going to freak.

"I brought some things for you from home."

When I look over at her I'm surprised that she doesn't meet my gaze. "What things?"

Everything I wanted I brought with me when I moved.

She glances my way before reaching for my hand. "A box of odds and ends and some photo albums."

I tug my hand free, not ready to think about the album she might be talking about. I need to change the subject, now.

"His parents are coming for dinner tonight," I blurt, loud enough for my dad to look back at me.

My mother goes ramrod straight and silent, which is never a good thing.

"Mama?" I ask.

Slowly, she turns her head so she can glare at me.

"They are going to meet me after twelve hours of travel in which my clothes have wrinkled and my skin has been dried out from two separate flights?"

Instead of answering her, I ask Noah, "How long do you think it will take to get to my house?"

"Thirty or so minutes. Want me to step on it?"

"Yes, please," I say, loud enough for him to hear, my eyes on my mom.

She pulls a mirror from her purse and starts powdering her nose.

"Your folks are coming over for dinner?" My dad asks Noah.

"Yes sir," he replies.

My dad nods, enjoying the sir. "Tell me about them."

Noah clears his throat and I feel guilty for my dad putting him on the spot. "Dad, no inquisitions please."

"No, no. It's fine," Noah assures me. "My mom and dad have been married for forty-one years. They were high school sweethearts. My family owns a local building supply store. My mom and dad ran it together for over twenty-five years and my older brother, Eli, runs it now."

"Do you have any other brothers or sisters?" Dad queries.

"There are five of us. Eli is the oldest, and then me; next is my brother Asher, my sister Abby and Gideon is the baby."

"Four boys," my mom says, sympathetically.

"We sure kept our parents on their toes," Noah laughs.

"From middle school on I felt like a glorified taxi driver with all of Finley's extracurriculars," my mom complains.

"Eli and I were driving once Abby and Gideon needed rides. My mom made sure we all pitched in."

"Your family sounds close." There's appreciation clear in dad's tone.

It was one thing he never liked about Allen. The Wiltshire's were not warm and inviting. They couldn't be bothered with meeting my parents. Even after our marriage, we rarely saw Allen's parents. It was sad how uninterested they were in spending any time together.

When we get to my house, my mom spends one minute looking at the first floor before racing upstairs, her carry-on in hand, to change and freshen up.

"Don't mind her." My dad motions after her as I stand. "She wants to make a good impression. Now, give me the grand tour."

I don't include the second floor in the tour to avoid interrupting my mom. When I show my dad the kitchen, I make a point to thank him for my appliances. Then I peek at the roast I have going in my crock-pot.

"It smells great kiddo," my dad says. "And, I can't get over all of the work you've done. Your mom and I were so scared when you moved out here. I'm relieved to see those fears were unfounded."

I give him a hug, my arms wrapping around his middle. "Thanks Dad." When I pull away my gaze moves to Noah. "I never would have managed a quarter of this without Noah's help."

"Thank you for taking such good care of my girl," my dad says to Noah.

Noah offers me his hand. I take it and he uses it to pull me close, tucking me into his side.

"It's been my pleasure," he answers my dad.

"Okay, okay!" my mom shouts, coming down the

stairs. "I no longer look a fright. Show me all of the work you've done."

Noah lets me go, staying in the kitchen with my dad.

I lead her to the dining room. "Noah and I built this table today. Ignore the legs. I was saving those to do with dad."

"Oh, your father will love that." She pauses, looking closer at the table. "You built this? It's gorgeous honey! Did you make the benches too?"

I shake my head. "Nope, I found those at a second hand shop."

She does a slow spin.

Other than the furniture in the center of the room, it's mainly empty. "You should add some crown molding and maybe a chair rail in here, that would really finish it off."

I move over to her and wrap my arm around her. "You like it?"

She hugs me back. "I do honey."

She oohs and ahs over each room on the first floor.

She lifts the decorative box from the top of my desk. "I love this little box." Opening the lid, she asks. "Why is it full of fortune cookie fortunes?"

Before I can answer her I hear Noah's bark of laughter from the hallway. I'm guessing he heard her question. Taking the box from her, I put the lid back on it and return it to the shelf of my desk.

My cheeks redden. "They're from all the times Noah and I had Chinese."

She smiles at me and wraps her arm around my waist. "I was in such a rush to powder my nose earlier. Do we have time for you to show me all the work you've done upstairs?"

"Of course mama."

My dad joins us when we head upstairs, Noah bringing up the rear. My mom already saw the master bedroom and bath when she freshened up. She followed us up to let my dad know once they got back to Texas she wanted one just like it.

Noah and I moved my stacked air mattresses to one of the spare bedrooms. I'm going to sleep there while my parents are in town.

"This place looks great sweetheart."

I can't help but look over his shoulder to lock eyes with Noah. He holds my gaze.

Last night he heard my no, fought the fear that prompted it and turned it into going slow. He's my dream man and I know deep down I don't deserve him. I'm terrified of the day he'll realize that as well. For now, I'll consider myself lucky he's more stubborn than I am.

A knock at the door, presumably Noah's parents, has us all moving back downstairs. Noah takes my hand and together we go to answer it.

"Hello," his parents greet when we open the door.

"Hi. Welcome. Please come in." I usher them through the door.

"We brought you a bottle of wine." Mrs. Thompson leans in to kiss my cheek as she passes it to me.

"Thank you," I say, looking at the label. "This will go perfectly with the roast."

His father inhales. "Smells fantastic."

"Thank you," I say again. "Come meet my parents."

Noah handles the introductions, "Mom, Dad, this is Tom and Georgiana Reeves, Mr. and Mrs. Reeves, this is my mom, Daisy, and my dad, Dennis Thompson."

"Please call me Georgie," my mom says, offering Noah's mom her hand.

After the introductions, Noah shows his parents around the house while my mom helps me in the kitchen. After my divorce, I got rid of everything that reminded me of Allen, including all of our kitchen tools, glasses, and dining sets. Even though my budget has been strapped, new plates, glasses, silverware, pots, pans, and a new serving set was a priority. I love to cook; I wasn't going to have Allen taint any part of it.

"These plates are gorgeous," my mom gushes, as we carry them out to set the table.

"I cleaned out their clearance section," I brag.

"Honey, just look at you," she says as we work side by side.

"What?" I ask, looking up.

She smiles and shakes her head. "You look so happy."

My lips part and I admit, "I am."

She rubs my arm. "I can tell."

I exhale in a rush. "I'm moving on."

"You sure are honey. My goodness. Allen would crap his pants if he saw Noah."

I lift my hand and scrunch my nose. "Don't bring up Allen."

She purses her lips. "You don't even want to hear the latest gossip?"

"What gossip?" I ask.

"That tart Allen left you for, left him for the lawyer who represented Allen in your divorce."

My mouth falls open. "What?"

She nods. "It's all over town. Serves him right, that rat bastard."

"Rat bastard?" Noah asks walking in. "Sounds interesting."

"It's not," I grumble, piercing my mother with a shut up glare.

"Everything okay?"

I shrug, and avoiding his question, ask, "Can you help me carry some stuff in from the kitchen?"

He nods his head. "Sure."

Once dinner is served, Noah sits at one end, with me at the other, our parents between us.

"This looks great kiddo," my dad says while Noah pours the wine.

Dinner goes great, even after politics come up. Thankfully, the conversation shifts to average low temperatures in the winter.

"Tomorrow your father and I are getting you an electric blanket," my mom says, her wide eyes on Dennis.

"Mom," I laugh. "You don't have to do that. Noah talked me into upgrading the furnace and we've put new insulation in every room we've worked on. As soon as we finish the spare bathroom, we're going to start the third floor. I promise I'm going to be warm this winter."

"And she has all these fireplaces," my dad adds. "She can make fires too."

"Oh can we have a fire while we're here?" My mom asks, no longer worried I'll freeze to death.

"Yes, Mom. We can have a fire tomorrow night if you want," I reply. Then I say, "Noah inspected all the fireplaces and helped me clean them."

My mom turns to stare at him. From the look in her eyes you'd think he wore a superhero cape.

"What are you going to do about the windows?" My dad asks, not aware he's walking into a minefield.

"I need to hold off until spring while I save up for them," I reply.

My dad looks at Noah. "Is that a wise decision?"

Noah wipes his mouth with his napkin before setting it on the table next to his plate. "I think Finley should do the windows before we do the guest bath."

"Noah," I warn.

"She'd only be able to do the first floor but the heat savings would be worth it."

"We already talked about this," I argue.

Noah shrugs and gestures around the room. "She would like to put them in all at the same time because that is the only way to guarantee they match perfectly. It's a valid concern so, we're going to add clear plastic insulation to the windows to get her through the winter."

"I bought insulated curtains too," I add, happy that while Noah disagreed with my choice he still heard my reasoning and backed me up on it.

"These windows aren't great," Mr. Thompson mutters. "But, waiting until spring to replace them should be fine. After that, it's the siding you'll need to start saving up for."

"Siding?" I squeak.

"We're going to repaint the existing siding next summer. That should give Finley another three to five years to save up to have it replaced," Noah answers.

"Noah said you bought the place outright. It's commendable you're doing the entire project without taking on a loan." Mrs. Thompson says.

"Thank you. It feels wrong to take any credit. This would have been a nightmare without your son."

"Stop saying that," Noah replies. "All I did was help speed up your timeline."

"You're not taking enough credit."

"I like this," my mom says.

"So do I," Mrs. Thompson agrees.

It's an effort not to roll my eyes, and I look over to see Noah holding back a laugh.

"What's for dessert?" My dad asks.

Pushing away from the table, I stand, grateful he changed the subject. "You'll see."

Mr. and Mrs. Thompson help clear the table, telling my parents to stay put since they traveled today. Noah kicks them out to help me with dessert.

The chocolate mousse trifle I made for Noah was so good, I found more recipes to try out. I start my coffeemaker while Noah ferries dessert forks and coffee cups to the dining room.

Once he's back, I ask, "Can you grab the dessert dishes please?"

"Only after I do this," he says, his voice husky and low, making my stomach tie in knots before he presses his lips to mine.

Like stepping into a warm bath, I melt into him. He steps closer, increasing our body contact and my fingers curl into his shirt. Our first kiss was last night. How is it possible I already feel this comfortable kissing him back? Then I remember our parents are in the next room and abruptly pull away, breaking our connection.

"How do you think it's going?" I ask, motioning with a tilt of my head to the dining room.

"You have to ask?" He teases.

He's right; it was silly to ask. Conversation has flowed easily all night, even considering the politics hiccup, which wasn't a big deal.

I move to my fridge and take out the trifle. "What do you think?"

His eyes widen. "It looks even better than the

chocolate one."

"It is pretty," I agree.

"Lead the way."

"I hope you all saved room," I set dessert on the table, feeling proud of myself.

"It almost looks too fancy to eat. Almost," my mom jokes.

"What is it?" Mrs. Thompson asks.

"It's a chocolate raspberry trifle. There's pound cake, raspberry preserves, white chocolate mousse, and raspberries."

My dad lifts his dessert plate. "Load me up honey."

I laugh and serve everyone a healthy portion.

"Marry her," Mr. Thompson grunts, still chewing.

I freeze.

Noah looks at me.

It's a joke. It's only a joke.

He smiles.

I gulp.

"Finley?" My mom calls.

My gaze moves from Noah to her. "Yes?"

She tilts her head to the side, her knowing eyes seeing way too much.

She nods, and gives me a small smile. "This is delicious sweetie."

I'm certain without an audience, she would have said something else. "Thanks."

We linger over coffee. My dad, Mr. Thompson and Noah all having seconds of the trifle. This being my second time in as many days with his parents, I already like them even more. I see so much of Noah in them. He's no nonsense like his dad and quiet and unassuming like his mom.

Before they leave, they invite us to their house for dinner before my parents head back to Texas. My parents happily accept. Noah walks them out, my folks and I wave from the front door.

We move from the dining room to my den. My mom cleans the kitchen, banning me from it since I cooked.

I put on a movie I think my dad will like and snuggle up next to Noah. I breathe in his cologne and let his warmth seep into me. What feels like moments later, he's gently shaking me awake. It appears our busy day caught up with me.

"Hmmm," I mumble.

He smiles down at me. "I'm going to hit the road. Do you need help getting upstairs?"

Twisting my neck I look for my parents then back to him when I see we're alone.

"They went up a little while ago," he explains.

"What time is it?" I ask.

"Late."

"Will you be okay to drive?"

He nods and shifts back as I sit up, rubbing at my eyes. "I'll walk out with you."

That has him shaking his head. "You will walk me to the door, kiss me, and then close it behind me so you can go upstairs and go to bed."

Frowning, I don't argue mainly because I'm tired. He offers me his hand and together we walk to the front door. Ever since we cleared the front yard it's been so much more convenient than going through the kitchen, unless I have groceries.

"Thank you for everything," I say, once we're standing

in my open doorway.

"Stop thanking me."

"Never," I reply, gripping his biceps and popping up on my tip toes to press my lips to his.

His arms band around me as he kisses me back.

When our kiss ends, he orders, "Sleep in, and no projects tomorrow. You need a day off to rest. Enjoy your visit with your parents."

"You're not coming over?"

His fingertips stroke down the side of my face. "Do you want me to?"

I nod.

"I didn't want to intrude on your time with them."

"You won't," I promise.

He leans down to kiss me again. I'm clutching at the soft fabric of his t-shirt before he's done. Each kiss is better than the last. Even half asleep I want to drag him back inside to keep kissing him.

It's the drive home ahead of him and the fact that my parents are upstairs that stops me.

"See you tomorrow."

I close the door behind him, leaning against it until I hear his truck pull away. Then I drag my exhausted butt upstairs.

As I settle down in my spare bedroom, I replay the night. There's no doubt in my mind my parents approve of not only my move but my budding relationship with Noah.

Yes, I may be thirty-five years old but I don't think I'll ever out grow wanting them to be proud of me. Then my thoughts shift to Noah. As sleep pulls me away, I can only hope my dreams will lead me back into his arms.

CHAPTER 14

Noah

"**Y**OU WERE SUPPOSED to take a day off."

"I told Finley to put me to work," her father argues.

"Doesn't it look good?" Finley asks, her hazel eyes pleading.

My gaze moves over the newly stained legs of the table we built yesterday. "It looks better than good."

"Really?" She presses, beaming a smile at me since she already knows.

I duck my head in assent.

"My mom wanted to check out that second hand store we got the benches and chairs at. Want to come with or stay here and hang out with my dad?"

I press the keys to my truck into her hand and kiss her temple. "Take it in case you find something that won't fit in your car. I'll keep your dad company."

"Are you sure?" She asks and I nod again.

"We won't be gone long."

173

"Go," I laugh, and then turn to her dad. "Has she shown you the shed?"

His eyebrows go up into his hairline. "Shed?"

Finley giggles as she leads her mother away.

"Come on," I reply. "I'll show you."

He follows me in to the backyard from the driveway. They had moved the table out to where we built it to stain it.

"This is where Finley found the door we used to make the table," I explain once we reach it.

His eyes move over the structure. "Do you think there's anything valuable in there?"

"It's hard to tell. If there is, it's buried under a mountain of junk."

He looks over at the dumpster that still sits at the end of her driveway. We've had it emptied once already so it's pretty empty at the moment.

"Want to clear out some of the junk while the womenfolk shop?"

I shrug. "Sure."

It's not long before the questions start.

"How old are you Noah?" He asks as we carry out a rotted armchair.

"I'm thirty-eight, sir."

"Thirty-eight and never married, why is that?"

I have to respect him for not pulling any punches. "I never met the right girl."

"Are you a playboy?"

I think he means player but instead of correcting him I answer his question. "No, sir."

He looks me up and down. "Call me Tom."

Then we get back to work.

"One, two, three," he counts and we toss the chair into the dumpster.

When we get back to the shed he drags a box to the door and motions for me to help him lift it and carry it to the driveway. He kneels next to it, opening it.

"What's in there?" I ask.

"Looks like utility bills from ten years ago."

As soon as he's done confirming there's nothing of value in the box we toss it in the dumpster as well. Box by box, we go through five before we find something interesting.

Her dad falls back onto his ass, laughing, "Finley is going to be pissed we were the ones who found this."

One thing Finley loved about this house was discovering things about it. She'll be annoyed that she wasn't here when we found it. It's an old binder full of stamps. Neither of us are stamp collectors so it could be worth nothing. But, it's better than old utility bills.

"Yeah she will," I smile. "I'll bring out the next box."

The stamps are our only find. Another four boxes of crap get thrown into the dumpster by the time Finley and her mom return.

"What are you guys doing?" She asks after parking.

Mr. Thompson gets to his feet. "Noah showed me your shed. We started clearing out some of the junk in it."

She comes closer. "Did you find anything?"

He bends down to pick up the binder and passes it to her. "Maybe yes, maybe no. You'll have to look them up on your computer to see if they're worth anything."

"No way," she yells, flipping through the pages.

"Did you ask them to help carry the hutch?" Her mom

asks.

"What hutch?" Her dad asks, looking at Finley.

"Oh," she replies, closing the binder and hugging it to her chest. "Mom bought me a hutch for the dining room."

"She did?" Tom asks, his voice rising at the end.

"It's an early birthday present," Mrs. Reeves explains.

"That's what I thought the kitchen appliances were," he mutters to no one in particular.

Still holding the binder to her chest, Finley leads us to the back of my truck. There, resting with its back to the bed is a vintage hutch. It's simple in construction, if I had to guess it's shaker or Amish. It's going to weigh a ton.

"How did you get it into the truck?" I ask.

Finley cringes. "Four men from the shop loaded it."

"Four?" Her dad groans.

"Grab the dolly."

When she comes back out, she isn't carrying the binder anymore.

"We'll need to make a ramp and cover the floor from the front door to where you want the hutch in the room," I tell her.

"I'll grab the plywood," Finley replies.

I smile after her before looking at Tom. "Spot me?"

He does better than that after we pull out the drawers, he helps me unload it and get it onto the dolly. Finley has the ramp set for us and with her mom, is laying newspaper sheets down to protect the floor.

Tom, stays beside me, his strength helping me from dropping the hutch as we push it up the ramp.

Once we have it in place, Finley and I carefully lower the legs to the ground.

"I hope you like it here because we are never moving

this thing again," her dad groans.

"I love it and love it right where it is. Thank you, thank you, thank you," she replies, hugging him.

His arms circle her, his face gentling as he kisses the top of her head. "You're welcome honey."

Mrs. Thompson and I pick up the sheets of newspaper while they hug. I take them all out to set in her recycling bin. Finley meets me at the front door.

"Is this taking today easy?" I ask, raising my eyebrows at her.

She manages to look adorable and guilty at the same time. I can already picture the crap she'll be talking me into in ten years. One thing I know for sure is that life will never be boring with her by my side. My chest tightens as my pulse starts to race at the realization I want it. I want forever with her.

"Are you going to try and relax for the rest of the day?" I ask.

She nods and grins up at me. I use it as an excuse to kiss her.

"Finley. I think your father pulled something. Do you have any pain killers?" Her mom asks, sticking her head out the kitchen door.

"Oh crap," Finley mutters before hurrying to her. "I have some upstairs."

I walk around the house to collect the wood we used for the ramp. By the time I have it and the dolly put away, they have her dad settled on the sofa with an ice pack.

"I'd rather have a beer." Mrs. Reeves hands him a glass of sweet tea.

"You shouldn't drink alcohol when you're on pain killers Tom," she replies.

"I'm so sorry about your back dad."

He waves his hand to shoo her. "I'll be fine as long as you put a shoot em up on the boob tube for me."

She finds a Western for him and motions for me to follow her mother and her out of the room.

Once we get to the room she's using as an office, she looks back toward her den. "I'm regretting not putting a door at the end of that hall now."

Her mother nods and then says, "We might have to leave."

I look from Finley to her mother and then back to Finley. "Am I missing something?"

That's when I hear a shouted, "Get him! Shoot him right between the eyes!" from her den.

Mrs. Reeves looks up at the ceiling.

"My dad gets loud when he watches Westerns," Finley explains unnecessarily.

"Do you need anything else for the house?" Her mom has to raise her voice for us to hear her over her father's shouts.

Finley grabs my hand and her mother's hand and pulls us to the front door.

Once we're outside she says, "I don't want you spending any more money on me."

"Not even for a couple light fixtures?" Her mom counters.

I bite back a smile as I watch Finley consider this, after a beat she answers, "Not even for some new light fixtures. Christine and Keith, the couple who live next door, said there were some good walking trails in the woods that border the neighborhood. The leaves are so pretty, Mom, people come from all over to see New England in the fall. Want to go for a walk?"

In a few years, Fin will start calling people who come

to see the fall leaves, leaf peepers, like a true Yankee.

Her mom grimaces. "Are you sure you wouldn't rather go shopping?"

"I'm sure Mom."

"There aren't any bears in those woods are there?"

Finley looks at me.

When I shrug, she takes a step closer to her mother and hugs her. "Are there bears in my woods?"

I frown and gesture towards the trees. "That's a decent sized forest, I don't know the exact acreage but if I had to guess I'd say there's a chance there're bears in there."

Finley looks at her mom. "I changed my mind about the light fixtures."

With wide eyes, her mom nods her head. "I'll go get my purse."

When her mom leaves, I ask, "Want to bring your table back in first? The legs should be dry."

"Okay," she agrees, stepping close to me and looking over her shoulder at the woods that surround her house on two sides.

"Hey," I say. "Don't get all scared about bears now. Sightings are rare in the city."

"How rare?"

"I'm not Google," I reply, taking her hand.

"Do they break into houses?"

I stop in my tracks and bend forward, my hand braced on my knee to laugh. She tries to shake her hand free but I hold tight.

"You don't have to laugh at me," she snaps.

Dropping her hand, I straighten and cup her face as I kiss her.

Lifting my head I start to laugh again. She smacks me in my stomach and storms away.

"I was just picturing a bear trying to pick a lock," I explain.

"It's not funny," she grumbles.

"It's a little funny," I argue.

She smirks and moves to one end of the table. I head to the other end and together we move it back into her dining room. From the moment we walk back into her house, her father's shouts become audible again.

"Has he always done that?" I ask when we get to my truck.

"He's been like this when it comes to Westerns for as long as I've known him," her mom, who Finley made sit up front, answers.

"My mom isn't allowed to watch the Patriots play," I reply.

"Why?" Finley and her mom ask in unison.

"She's bad luck for football," I reply.

"That's crazy," Finley snorts from the backseat.

"It's the truth," I reply. "My brother played football and he and my dad banned her from coming to his games. I played hockey so it pissed him off she came to my games."

"What does your mom do when they're watching football?" Finley asks.

I meet her eyes in the rearview mirror. "She won't tell us."

"She probably watches the game from somewhere else."

"She might," I reply with a grin. "But, if she does she'd never admit to it."

FIX HER UP

When we get to the store, Finley lets her mom talk her into a simple chandelier for the dining room, and two matching ceiling fixtures to go in the kitchen and the room she uses as her office.

"You should leave your desk in there and make that room a library," her mom suggests, as we walk out of the store.

"A library?" Finley repeats, surprise evident in her tone. "The only books I collect these days are cook books and I store those in my kitchen. When I read, I use an app on my phone."

"That's a travesty," her mother replies. "There is nothing," she looks over at me and repeats, "nothing better than holding an actual book in your hands."

"Until you have to travel and your carry on bag weighs a ton because of all the books you packed."

"Your argument would hold more weight if you traveled sweetie," she teases.

Finley and I spent hours getting to know each other as we worked on her house. In all the topics we covered, travel never came up.

"Do you like to travel?" I ask.

She shoves one of the light fixtures onto the bed of my truck. "Yes and no."

I unload the other fixture. "You're going to need to elaborate."

Her mouth twists. "I don't enjoy the getting from point A to point B part but once I'm in point B, I like it."

I shut the tailgate. "Any places you'd like to see someday?"

She waits until we're in the truck to reply, "Greece. I'd like to go to Greece someday."

"I've been to Crete. It was—"

181

She cuts me off. "You've been to Crete?"

I meet her eyes in the rear view mirror and nod while her mother chuckles from the passenger seat.

"What was it like?" Finley asks.

"It's almost as beautiful as New Hampshire in the fall," I reply.

"Come on," she groans. "Leaves changing colors can't compare to the history of Crete."

"But the leaves are so stunning," her mother argues.

"Crete is the birthplace of Zeus," Finley shouts.

"Which light fixture do you want to install first?" I ask, hoping to change the subject.

"Why did you go to Greece?" Finley asks, ignoring my question.

"I spent a summer backpacking through Europe."

"Where else did you go?" She asks.

"I hit all the major cites; London, Paris, Berlin, Amsterdam, Barcelona, Lisbon, Venice and Crete."

"That sounds amazing," she breathes.

I laugh. "There was a whole lot of that getting from point A to point B part that you don't like."

"He's got you there," her mom jokes.

"Were you all by yourself?" Finley asks, undeterred.

"I was not," I admit and leave it at that.

"A woman?" She guesses.

"Yes," I reply.

Unbidden, my thoughts are flooded with memories of Candace.

"What happened?" Her mom asks.

"She stayed in Crete," I reply.

"She . . . why would she do that?" Finley asks.

I park. "To be with her new boyfriend I suppose."

Finley's face is illuminated by the interior light when I open my door. I do not miss her lips parting.

She moves to my side the moment she's out. "I'm sorry I asked."

I silence her with a kiss. "We didn't date that long and it was years ago."

"Sure?" She asks.

I nod. "Which light do you want to put up first?"

She grins. "The dining room one."

Mrs. Reeves opens and then holds the door open for us as we carry the boxes in.

"It's quiet," Finley whispers, looking at her mom.

Mrs. Reeves presses her index finger to her lips and then silently walks back to the den. Finley and I set the boxes down.

"He's asleep," her mom whispers once she returns.

"We should hold off on installing the light," Finley says in a hushed tone.

I nod in agreement. "What do you want to do instead?"

"Georgie? Finley? Where are you?" Her father shouts from the den.

I cringe. "Did I wake him?"

Mrs. Reeves shakes her head. "Coming."

I tip my head towards the boxes. "Install back on?"

"I'll grab my toolbox."

Nothing sexier than a woman who knows how to use tools. Since I taught Finley myself, her toolbox a gift from me, she knows more than most.

This install will be easier than most. When Finley had

the entire house rewired, she was smart enough to have each room prepped for ceiling fixtures.

When we replaced the drywall, we put in ceiling boxes to brace any future light fixtures or ceiling fans Finley got. We marked each spot with a gold star sticker. Normally, I would have used painter's tape. The gold stars were Finley's idea. She didn't want blue painters tape on her ceilings while she saved up for fixtures and, she thought the gold stars were funny.

Since we're alone, I say, "Your parents are cool."

Her face softens and she looks toward the den. "They're the best."

We move the furniture out of the way and set up ladders under the gold star.

"Do you mind an audience?" Tom asks from the doorway.

"Not at all sir. How's your back feeling?"

He shrugs. "It's been better."

"Dad, you should try out my bath. It's amazing."

"You wanna give me a sponge bath?" He asks Mrs. Reeves, wagging his eyebrows.

Finley's nose wrinkles.

She turns to me with wide eyes. "Can I drill?"

I point up. "We'll need to cut a hole first."

"Oh right," she laughs.

I get my saw and make a hole to expose the ceiling box we installed and the wiring the electrician put in.

Without walking her through it, I let Finley take the lead on the install. It's the perfect opportunity for her to showcase all she's learned for her parents. She has a couple of questions along the way but other than holding the fixture up for her, she does all the work.

After her mom gives her a light bulb, Finley asks, "Want to flip the switch and see if it works?"

"Let there be light!" Tom cheers when the bulb lights up.

The look on Finley's face is one I'll never forget. She blossoms under his praise. "She's incredible," I say and watch her smile grow wider.

"She takes after her mother," Mrs. Reeves puts in.

It takes even less time to put in the fixture in the kitchen. Once they're in, and the mess we made putting them in is cleaned up, we all move to the den.

"Is it time to make the fire yet?" Her mom asks as soon as we sit down.

CHAPTER 15

Finley

WITH A BIT more force than necessary, I close out my last ticket for the day. Before I can celebrate, there's a knock on my front door. Since I'm not expecting anyone, I hesitate, staring at the door for a moment before standing. I don't get a lot of visitors and I almost never get unexpected ones.

Noah has a key, not that he's spent the night or the physical side of our relationship has gone past kissing yet. He has a key because my parents thought it was silly he didn't have one. Their reasoning was more sensible than romantic. They argued it would give them piece of mind to know he could get to me if I ever needed him.

Heaven forbid the fact that I've only known him months and there's no guarantee our relationship will go anywhere. After they left, he offered to give me the key back but my mom can tell if I'm lying so I made him keep it. That was over a month ago and I have no plans on asking for it back.

It can't be Abby because she would have texted to say

she was dropping by. Pushing away from my desk I hurry to the door. When I open it, it's shock that keeps me from slamming it as soon as I see who's standing on my doorstep.

"Aren't you going to invite me in?" Allen, my ex-husband asks.

Allen, the man I thought I was going to spend the rest of my life with; the man who also traded me in for a woman more than a decade younger than me; and the man I never thought I'd see again.

Concerned that I'm not only experiencing delusions but that said delusion is talking to me I start to close the door.

"Finley," he shouts, throwing his hand out to keep the door open.

"You are not here," I snap.

"I thought you'd be happy to see me."

I blink and then blink again. He's here; Allen is really here.

The urge to punch him right in the chin is strong. Why in the hell would he think I ever wanted to see him again?

"I don't want to talk to you or see you," I shout.

He rears back as if struck. What he doesn't do is remove his hand from my door.

A car door slams. "Is there a problem here?"

Allen looks over his shoulder while I look past him to watch as Noah approaches.

"Noah."

Allen's head twists to look at me. "You know this man?"

Noah doesn't give me time to answer; he pulls Allen

off my doorstep.

"Unhand me," Allen shrieks, shaking off Noah's hold.

As soon as he's free, Noah moves to place himself between us and ask, "Who is this guy?"

"My *ex*-husband," I reply.

Noah's eyebrows shoot up and he glares at Allen. "Why are you here?"

Allen's face twists. "I don't have to explain myself to you."

Noah's shoulders give a slight lift and he turns, stepping into the house. He tucks me into his side, and with his gaze locked on Allen's, he shuts the door.

I look up at him, fighting back a smile.

A second later Allen starts knocking on the door. "I'm not leaving until I talk to Finley!" He yells through the door and I find myself once again grateful for the distance between me and my neighbors.

"Do you want to talk to this guy?" Noah asks, his eyes shifting just once to the door before returning to me.

I shake my head.

He gives me a lopsided grin. "I'd ask how your day was but . . ." He trails off and we both chuckle lightly.

Allen knocks again. "Finley!"

I tilt my head back and stare up at my ceiling.

"Anything interesting up there?" Noah teases.

I shake my head. "Nope."

Allen continues to knock.

"Is he going to go away?"

I close my eyes. "I have no idea. I don't know what he wants."

"Only one way to find out," He winks, not seeming at

all bothered by Allen's presence.

"Finley," Allen shouts.

"Fine," I grumble, tipping my head back down to look at the door.

Noah opens the door and before Allen can say anything, says, "You stay right there. Say what you came to say and then leave."

Allen squints in confusion as he focuses on me. "Who is this man?"

My eyes travel over him. This isn't the first time I've seen his annoyance. Over the years of our marriage it's a look I was all too familiar with. His dark brown, so dark it looked black, hair is perfectly styled and recently trimmed. He had a standing biweekly appointment at a salon, not a barber, a salon. He was more particular about his appearance than I ever was about mine.

It would kill him to know that either all his knocking or when Noah pulled him off of my doorstep, wrinkled his button up shirt. Appearance always mattered so much more to him than it ever did to me. It wasn't only the way I dressed or the fact that I wasn't obsessed with makeup or getting my nails done.

He hated my job, hated that I worked from home and enjoyed it. Standing there, in a wrinkled shirt, dress slacks, and loafers, I wonder what I ever saw in him. With a start I realize his power over me is gone, that emotional poison purged from my body.

"This is my boyfriend, Noah," I reply.

"You're seeing someone?" He asks incredulously, a wounded expression on his face.

"Yeah, she is," Noah mutters, draping his arm across my shoulders.

"But our divorce has only been final for—"

"Are you kidding me?" I snap, cutting him off. "You're offended I waited for our divorce to be final to start dating? We were still married when you started dating."

"It was a mistake." As if belittling and then cheating on your wife of ten years was no big deal.

"A mistake?" I whisper.

"I want you back," he replies.

He said he wanted me back. There was a time I would have jumped at the opportunity to reconcile. I thought the breakup of our marriage was my fault, that I somehow drove him away.

Noah stiffens beside me.

"What?" I ask.

"I've come to win—" he starts.

"She heard you," Noah snaps.

"I just didn't believe you," I add.

Never in a million years would I ever have imagined I'd see Allen and Noah together. The side-by-side comparison does no favors for Allen. It's hard to remember what attracted me to him in the first place. There's a hardness to his face I never noticed before, as if his mouth was always ready to deliver some criticism and froze that way.

Allen tilts his head to the side. "Why is it so hard to believe?"

That question surprises me. At this point, looking back on our marriage, it's harder to believe he loved me at all. Nothing I ever did was right or good enough for him.

"You don't even like me," I reply.

"I love you," he scoffs.

"You have no idea what love is," I argue. "If you did,

you would understand."

"Was there anything else you needed to say?" Noah asks.

Allen glares at him.

Noah looks at me and repeats his question, ignoring Allen. "Was there anything you needed to say to him?"

Since our divorce was finalized I've probably imagined a million different things I'd say to him. In my head I'd ask him what I did wrong, or why he couldn't love me the way I was. Staring at him, I know even if I ask those questions nothing he could say would ever make me trust him again. More importantly, I no longer care.

My gaze moves to Allen. "I never want to see you again."

"Finley," he argues but he doesn't get far.

"You heard the lady," Noah mutters, before shutting the door in his face.

Allen immediately starts knocking on the door again.

"Was he always like that?" Noah asks.

My eyes are on the door. "I never saw it before, but yes, yes he was."

He moves in front of me, breaking my eye contact with the door and presses his lips to mine. For a brief, blissful, moment, everything else fades away, including Allen's incessant knocking.

When Noah breaks our kiss, he says, "Babe, you rebounded up."

"You are not a rebound," I snap.

He grins, his smile quickly fading as Allen continues to knock. "Can I kick his ass now?"

I have no love lost for Allen but it's been a long time

since I wished him physical harm. "Is there another way we can get him to leave?"

Noah pulls his phone from his back pocket and moves his thumb over the screen before lifting it to his ear. "Hey Marc. Got time to do me a favor?"

I listen as he explains our situation and then rattles off my address to whoever is on the other end.

"Who was that?" I ask.

"A buddy of mine is a sheriff," he replies.

My eyes widen.

He shrugs. "Marc's a good guy. We went to high school together."

"Will he arrest Allen?" I ask.

He smirks, shaking his head. "Only if he's an idiot and doesn't leave after Marc asks."

"I can't believe he came here," I grumble.

"He's figuring out he made a mistake letting you go. Too bad for him that's not a mistake I'll make."

"How are you so sure?" I ask, stepping closer to him.

He frames my face with his hands, his warm gaze consuming me. "I was never expecting to meet the most beautiful woman I've ever seen when Abby sent me here that day. You intrigued me from the start. Then you worked your way under my skin. We spend hours together everyday and our time together is always the best part of my day."

"Really?" I breathe.

He kisses me, dropping his hands from my face to wrap his arms around me.

"You called the police?" Allen shouts.

"Sounds like Marc is here," Noah remarks, lifting his head.

I press my lips together. He surprises me by not moving away.

"Should we go?" I ask.

He frowns, before releasing me. When he turns, he offers me his hand. Slipping my hand into his I wonder how long he'll have to keep cleaning up my messes.

"You're presence is not needed," Allen argues, his back to us.

It gives me a chance to check out Noah's friend. Marc's name has come up more than once as we got to know each other. Noah even showed me a picture of the baby his wife just had.

"Yo Noah," Marc greets, lifting his chin. He then directs his attention to Allen. "Sir, the owner of this property has asked you to leave. If you refuse to, I will arrest you for trespassing."

Allen turns to me. "Trespassing? Is this truly necessary Finley?"

"It is. She told you she never wanted to see you again so yeah, since you didn't leave and have been banging on her door and shouting."

"I wasn't talking to you," Allen huffs.

"I want you to leave," I say and they all look at me.

Allen takes a step toward me and both Noah and Marc jump into action. Noah shifts in front of me blocking Allen from reaching for me as Marc comes up behind him and pulls him away.

"Alright buddy. It's time for you to leave." As he leads Allen away, he looks over his shoulder. "Noah, you and Finley go inside."

"Are you sure we shouldn't stay out here?" I ask.

Noah shakes his head. "Marc's got this."

My brows furrow as I look back to see Allen gesturing

toward me. Trusting Noah, I let him guide me back inside.

As soon as the door closes behind us, I start to pace. "I cannot believe this."

"He's a dick."

"Still want to kick his ass?" I joke.

That makes him smile. "I bet I could get Marc to look the other way."

"Yeah?" I ask.

He nods, taking my hand and tugging me toward the kitchen. "Yep, I introduced him to his wife."

"You did?" I laugh.

He nods. "She knows Abby. Marc saw them out and asked about her. I got Abby to give me a heads up the next time they went out and Marc and I just happened to show up at the same place."

"You're a good friend," I reply.

He opens the fridge and pulls out a beer, opening it and passing it to me before grabbing another for himself. "Marc's a good guy. I'm glad things worked out for them."

I take a sip of my beer. It dawns on me then that I'd still be trying to get rid of Allen if Noah had not shown up when he had. The way Allen wouldn't let me close the door makes me wonder if he would have forced his way inside. Just the thought of him inside this place turns my stomach.

It's funny how much has changed.

"Are you okay?" Noah asked.

I bob my head. "Yes. Confused, but okay."

His eyebrows furrow. "Just confused?"

I shrug.

He shakes his head. "He shows up here unexpectedly

and doesn't leave when you ask him to, that's not normal."

He's right, my lips part and he cups the back of my head.

"Was he, did he—" He pulls in a breath. "Did he ever hurt you?"

I shake my head. "No. No, never." I pause and then amend, "physically."

I watch as his eyes slowly close, the weight of my words a blow. His chest rises and falls three times before his eyes open and he reaches for me, pulling me into a hug.

I melt into him, letting his familiar scent and hold sooth me. "Not all abuse is physical."

He stiffens his arms squeezing me tightly before he asks. "What did he do?"

With my cheek pressed to his chest, my arms folding up between us, still holding my beer, I reply, "I never did anything right. I never looked right, said the right things, or cared about the things he thought were important. It was like he was emotionally poisoning me."

"Finley," he whispers, feeling in his tone.

My name on his lips is a balm. Since I've met Noah I've been nothing but myself. He likes me for me, and not what I look like on his arm at a party. He gets that I'm happier at home cuddled up on the couch watching a movie with him than I'll ever be out at a fancy club.

He likes that I want to take care of myself and renovate this place. Even if I had tons of money I would have wanted to do the work myself. He not only gets that, he's the same way. Not once has he tried to change me or judged me for the things that interest me. No, all he did was offer me his help.

There's a knock on the door.

"Stay here," Noah orders.

I ignore him and move with him toward the hallway to the front door. He stops, frowning down at me before accepting me for who I am again and offering me his hand.

It's Marc. I peer around him and see no Allen.

"Can I come in?" Marc asks.

"Sure," I reply and then offer, "would you like something to drink?"

"A glass of water would be great. Thanks," he replies.

Noah shows him to the den while I get his drink and Noah's beer.

"Noah's been texting me pictures of all the work you two have done on this place. Seeing it in person makes it even more impressive. Don't take it personal if I ban Brianna from coming over here. She sees this place she'll have me knocking down walls."

I reach across my milk crate coffee table to pass him his glass. "Thank you, and thank you for your help today."

Reaching behind me to feel for the sofa, I slowly sit beside Noah. "What did he say to you?"

"He seems convinced you'll take him back."

"He's the one who left me," I argue, my eyes moving to Noah's.

His arm moves around my shoulders, pulling me close. "He's messed up in the head."

"I haven't even heard anything from him in months."

"Nothing?" Marc asks. "No emails, letters, texts, or phone calls?"

I shake my head. "Nothing."

"Did you change your telephone number when you moved?"

I shake my head again. "I didn't"

"What about your parents? Has he been in touch with them at all?" He asks.

"I don't think so but I can call my mom and ask," I offer.

He nods. "You should do that now."

My eyes widen. "Okay."

My phone is in my purse, which is currently sitting on the kitchen countertop. I feel their eyes on my back as I walk away. Once I'm in the kitchen, with my phone to my ear, I take another drink of my beer and I listen to it ring.

"Hey honey," my mom greets. "How's my girl?"

"Um, Allen was just here," I reply.

"What?" She shrieks.

"Yeah," I reply. "Noah is here. One of his friends is a sheriff and asked if Allen has been in touch with you or dad recently."

She doesn't reply and I tap the outside edge of my fist onto my concrete countertop.

"Mom?"

"We didn't want to worry you," she cries.

"Tell me everything," I reply and then jump when I feel Noah's arms wrap around me from behind.

My free hand comes up to hug his arms to me as I listen to my mom.

"He started coming around after we got home. He wanted to speak to you. Was saying that he made a mistake and it was his fault you left Texas. He thought we would want his help in convincing you to move back home."

"Mom," I groan. "Why did you keep this from me?"

"Your father and I didn't want you to worry. We never imagined he would come out there."

"How did he find me?" I ask.

"I don't know honey. Maybe he found out from your boss," she replies.

"Can you think of anything else that he said?"

There's another pause before she admits, "He sent your dad some emails."

"Mom," I sigh. "Can you please forward them to me?"

"I will honey. I'm so sorry."

"I love you mom."

After she echoes her love, I end the call and set my phone down.

"So, your ex has been in touch with them," Noah remarks.

"In person, over the phone and emails," I answer.

He kisses the top of my head. "I'd be more comfortable if you stay at my place until he's back in Texas."

I turn in his arms and hug him.

"Come on," Noah encourages. "We should tell Marc what your mom said.

After relaying the conversation to Marc, I add, "I asked her to forward the emails to me."

"I'll grab your laptop," Noah replies.

CHAPTER 16

Noah

"COME HERE," I mutter, opening my arms.

She approaches the edge of the bed, and puts a knee to it before making her way to me. As soon as she's close, she crawls into my arms.

"I want to go home," she murmurs, and then pulls back to look me in the eyes. "Not that I don't appreciate everything that you're doing for me."

"Shut up," I laugh, putting my hand to the back of her neck and pulling her lips down to mine.

She settles back against me, sinking into our kiss. As far as I'm concerned, I owe her ex. The emails he sent her mom and dad made him sound completely unhinged. He talked about Fin like their divorce had never happened, as though she was still his wife and he couldn't understand why her parents weren't helping him find her.

What Fin's parents had also kept from her was the fact that they had been in touch with Allen's parents. They were going to get him the help he needed to stop fixating on Finley. As good as that all sounded, as long as he was here and not in Texas, I wasn't letting her out of my sight.

Since there wasn't anything threatening in the emails there wasn't much we could do. After talking it through, Finley didn't argue with staying with me. She also didn't blink when I asked her to sleep with me in my room, rather than the spare.

Ever since we got back to my house, she's been down. She brought a glass of wine with her into the bathroom and took a long time getting ready for bed. I heard her crying through the door. She's letting that asshole mess with her head.

That ends now.

I've done everything I can think of to cheer her up.

Well, almost everything.

It's time to kick things up a notch.

She's here, in my arms and I'm once and for all making her forget about her asshole ex.

I turn, flipping her onto her back. She blinks up at me and then presses her lips together, instantly parting them when I kiss her again. She smells like fresh picked flowers and tastes like wine.

Her arms coil around my neck as I deepen our kiss, her tongue brushing against mine. Her hips press up against mine and I grind into her.

She tugs at my shirt and I lean back to pull it off. Before I can cover her with my body again, her hands glide over my chest. They rest on my pecs for a few beats, and then continue to roam.

My gaze is on her face. Her eyes are locked on her hands, watching them as they move over my skin.

"I've thought about doing this so many times," she

murmurs.

Her touch is delicate, her fingers warming my skin. There's an addictive quality to the way her hands move over me. I never want her to stop.

She moves them around my waist to my back. I lean closer, hovering over her. With her hands on my back, she pulls me even closer. Then her hands travel up my back and into my hair. I take her lips again, and again.

Bracing myself on one forearm, I do some exploring myself, my free hand moving to stroke the side of her waist.

My lips move to her jaw and then down her neck. Her pulse ripples against my tongue. I continue downward, to the V-neck of her cotton sleep shirt.

The swell of her breasts is a temptation I can no longer resist. My hand moves up from her waist, my thumb brushing the underside of her breast. Her back arches as I kiss her nipple through the fabric of her shirt.

With her hands in my hair, she holds me to her breast. I suck her nipple into my mouth, my other hand moving to palm her other breast.

"Noah," she groans, the sound of her need going straight to my cock. It strains against my boxers, pulsing with need.

My thumb strokes her nipple and it tightens into a hard bud. My mouth moves to her other breast, taking it into my mouth as my other hand moves to the hem of her shirt. I want to feel her skin against mine.

Her hands leave my hair as she helps me uncover her. I've seen her skin before; a bare shoulder here, a glimpse of her waist there, never this much.

"You're so fucking beautiful," I breathe.

Then I drop my mouth to her. She writhes beneath

me, her back arching, her hips undulating, her hands going to the waist of my pajama bottoms. Her skin is silken; the feel of it against mine has my nerves tingling with pleasure.

I shift away. I plan to give her plenty of time to explore me.

Later.

Now, it's my turn.

Her skin is so soft, I kiss my way down her stomach, lingering over her belly button as I undress her.

As soon as I drop her clothes to the floor, I spread her legs and look at her. Shifting on the bed she tries to close her legs, blush tingeing her cheeks as she looks away.

"Trust me?" I ask.

Slowly, her gaze moves to lock with mine before she nods, letting her legs fall open for me. She's completely bare and so beautiful my chest aches just looking at her. Her fingers nervously grab and twist at the sheets.

I hold her gaze, assuring her with my eyes. Her eyes drop to my mouth and she lets out a small surprised laugh when I blow a raspberry on her thigh. That's all the warning I give her before I lower my head and finally taste her. As I take her with my tongue, I watch her reaction.

Her laughter quickly shifts to moans of pleasure. With parted lips, her hands go to her breasts where she begins to squeeze them and tug at her nipples. She isn't just beautiful; she is the absolute sexiest woman I have ever seen.

"Noah," she cries out through her orgasm, right before her legs begin to tremble around my head.

I continue to lap at her. Her chest rises and falls as she struggles to catch her breath. Licking my lips I lift my head. She sits up, her hands coming to either side of my face and she pulls my mouth to hers.

She moans against my lips as she tastes herself on my tongue. I sit up as well, tugging her and flipping us over so she can straddle my lap, my arms banding around her waist. My chest tightens as she peers down at me.

Her hands push between us and into my pants, wrapping her hand around my hard length.

"I need you," she pleads as we kiss, her hand stroking me.

I reach past her to my bedside table. Tugging open the drawer, I pull out a box of condoms. Behind her back I rip the box in half and quickly open the first packet I grasp.

Finley moves her hand as I sheath myself. Once it's on, I shift my pants as far as I can down my thighs. While I do this, she takes me in her hand again, lines herself above me and then lowers herself onto me.

"Fuck," I growl as I sink into her.

Even through the condom, her heat coats me. My heart thunders wildly in my chest as I stare at her. I've wanted her for so long. Spent night after night wrapping my hand around my cock imagining what it would feel like to finally be inside her.

She's a goddess, all pink from my touch with her dark hair falling around her. My hands go to her ass, raising her, immediately pulling her back down to fill her again, and again, and again.

Our mouths fuse, her hands in my hair, her breasts pressed to my chest. Lifting her, I roll her to her back before covering her body with mine. Our eyes lock, her hand reaching up to stroke my face as I ease into her. God, she feels so fucking good, the best I've ever had.

Her legs wrap around my waist as I push my hands under her to grip her ass. I thrust into her and push my face into her neck.

"Don't stop," she begs.

Never.

I will never stop wanting her.

"Right there," she moans. "Right . . . right there."

Hell, hearing how close she is turns me on even more. I slam into her as she clutches me tightly, screaming my name again. It's her orgasm, and the way she pulses against my cock that is my undoing.

"Fuck," I breathe as I spill into her.

Before I collapse on her, I twist so we end up on our sides, our bodies slick with sweat.

Her gaze locks with mine. "Wow."

Wow is right.

I grin and press my mouth to hers. She returns my kiss and I kick myself for waiting this long.

"Let me take care of the condom," I mutter, pulling away and getting rid of my pajama bottoms.

Finley seems to enjoy the show, blatantly watching me. My eyes return the favor. When I see the mess of condoms around her, I bite back a laugh. Finley looks around herself and grins before she pulls the destroyed box out from under her side and tosses it off of the bed.

She shifts up onto her elbow, resting her head on her palm to watch me as I walk toward my bathroom. It's going to take a lot longer than one night to do everything I want to her.

When I get back to bed I pull her into my arms.

She snuggles into me. "That was incredible."

"Oh, I'm just getting started with you," I promise,

kissing her neck.

"Wait, wait," she groans, pushing me away.

"What?" I pout, reaching for her.

She grins. "We need to talk about what just happened."

I hold my head in my hand. "Like a performance evaluation? I say we both earned a ten out of ten."

Her smile widens and I wrap my hand around the back of her neck, pulling her to my waiting lips. "Need a replay?"

With her lips against mine, she says, "no, this is important."

Groaning, I shift onto my back, tugging her half on top of me, her hair falling around us. "You have my undivided attention."

"Do you think this is a good idea?"

I frown at her question. "Us?"

She tilts her head to the side and presses her hand to my cheek. "Not us being an us but us getting physical this soon."

"This soon?" I tease.

Her brows come together. "We've only been officially dating just over a month."

"I've wanted my mouth between your legs since the first day we met," I counter.

She presses her lips together and I shift her further onto me before wrapping my arms around her. Her skin is so soft, her body so addictive, I'm not sure I'll be able to keep my hands off her.

She ducks her face into my neck. "I can't believe we did that."

"Did that?" I repeat, confused.

"Never mind." Her shy reply comes too quickly.

I don't let it go. "Do you mean me eating you?"

"Let's talk about something else," she deflects.

I shift away from her and push her hair back from her face so I can see her eyes. "You have nothing to be shy about. I loved it. Hell, I'm already thinking about the next time I can get my mouth on you."

"Noah," she gasps.

I grin at her. "You want, you can crawl up here, hold onto the headboard and I promise you I'll make you scream."

"Oh my God," she breathes.

With wide eyes she tries to turn and hide how she blushes. Stopping her, I take the opportunity to kiss her. She doesn't hesitate long before she's kissing me back.

All too soon she stops again. "Stop trying to seduce me. We haven't finished talking yet."

My rising semi starts to deflate. She's naked, lying on top of me. Any conversation we have will not be getting my full attention.

"Are you sure this isn't too soon?"

My hands slide up her back and then slowly back down, hopefully relaxing her. "I've wanted you for so long. Trust me, I don't think we're rushing. But, since you're the one who's worried, it sounds like *you* think we are rushing."

She presses her lips together and I keep rubbing her back.

It doesn't take her long to quietly admit. "My divorce hasn't even been finalized for a year."

"Are you still in love with him?" I ask even though I already know the answer.

"No," she snaps, her lip curling.

"Exactly," I explain. "Your marriage is over. I don't have an issue with you being divorced, do you?"

She stares at me before surprising me by saying, "I feel bad for being divorced. I hate that you're settling for me."

I lift a hand to press the bridge of my nose. "Settling for you?"

Her shoulder dips as she gives me a noncommittal shrug.

"I do not feel like I'm settling for you," I promise. "If anything, I think you were made for me. I have never," I repeat my last word for emphasis, "*never* met anyone that I've wanted not only physically, but in every way, the way I want you. We're together every single day. Have I given you any reason to doubt the way I feel about you?"

She shakes her head and I keep going. "You're the one with the concerns here. Do you think being together is a mistake?"

She shakes her head. "No. No, I don't."

I lift my brows. "Sure?"

She lowers her head to my chest. "I'm a head case."

My hands stop moving on her so I can shift her onto me fully. "You've gone through more changes in a short period of time than most."

She nods in agreement.

"How about we get away for a weekend?"

"And go where?"

"My brother Asher has a small cabin on his property. I can call him and see if we can use it."

"He's the one that lives on a lake, right?" She asks.

"Yep." My hands shift into her hair as I pull her face close to mine. "I'll tell you all about it later."

She laughs at my blatant subject change and I kiss her anyway. Her laughter dies as she kisses me back. She pushes me onto my back and I willingly let her.

Then, she explores. Her hands move over me like a silken caress. She shifts up to sit, straddling me, grinding against me as her hands and lips move downward.

"Damn that feels good," I groan when she eases herself between my legs and begins stroking me.

Shoving a pillow behind my head, I watch her. She licks her lips before lowering her head and taking me into her mouth, her dark hair falling around her.

Pushing her hair to the back of her head, I fist it as she works me.

Jesus, does she work me.

I'll never need to watch porn again, if I ever need to take care of myself in the future, all I'll need to do is recall this moment.

She locks eyes with me as she drags her tongue across my cock. Then she takes me deep, hollowing her cheeks as she sucks me.

My fist in her hair tightens, my hips instinctively pushing upward. If she keeps this up I'm going to be coming down her throat soon.

"Come here," I growl, my hand leaving her hair as I bend forward to grab her under her arms.

She reaches for one of the condom packages that still litters my bed. My hands roam as I kiss her, cupping her breasts and tweaking her nipples. She opens the condom and stretches it down my length before lowering herself onto me.

It's the second time I've been inside her. I assumed

the emotions I felt the first time we made love were heightened because I've wanted her for so long. The intense bliss I feel with our connection is only stronger this time.

She rides me, breaking our kiss and straightening her back as she takes me. My hands grip her waist, lifting her and then lowering her as my hips punch upward. Need drives me to take her harder, faster.

Fuck, as hot as it is to watch her ride me, I need to pound into her. Turning her onto her back, I lean back and grab her ankles.

She throws her hands back and grips the headboard as I thrust into her.

"Yes," she moans.

Her breasts bounce each time I slam into her. I can't take my eyes off her. She's stunning, milky cream skin and dark brown hair spread across my pillow.

"Don't stop," she pleads.

This is the second time tonight she's said this.

I bend over her, folding her in half, going deeper, thrusting harder.

"I won't stop. I'll never stop. I'll make you come so many times you won't be able to get out of this bed ever again."

That does it. With a breathy groan she cries out. I tumble after her, burying my face into her neck as I growl out my release.

She smacks my arm after I collapse on her. "You're squishing me."

Rolling to my back, she follows, splaying out across my chest.

We lay there for a few moments catching our breath before she looks up at me. "Can we swim in the lake?"

I'm guessing that's a yes to going away for the weekend. "It won't be warm enough until next summer."

Her head pops up. "Can we ice skate on it?"

I lean up to kiss her, feeling light and happy that she wants to go away and sounds excited. "It should freeze over in January. We can go back then and skate on it. This trip we can go for a hike around the lake. It's pretty this time of year with all the leaves."

Her eyes get all dreamy. "Okay."

I sit up and pull her with me. "Let's take a bath."

"Not a shower?"

I shake my head. "I want to hold you."

When we reach the bathroom, I get rid of the condom before twisting on the water.

She smiles up at me, pressing her palm to my chest and popping up onto her toes to offer me her lips. She's surprised me by how comfortable she is with her body. Not once has she tried to hide herself from me. When I'm by myself, I like to sleep naked. I'm looking forward to doing it with her naked body wrapped around mine tonight.

We kiss as the tub fills with water. Once it's full, Finley climbs in first, making room for me to ease in behind her. She settles her back to my chest and I hug her to me. Her head rests against my shoulder, her face turning so she can kiss my neck.

"My legs feel like jelly."

I take that as the compliment intended and rub my shin against her. "They feel great to me."

She laughs and I'm reminded that only hours ago she was stressed out over her ex. Now she's sated and laughing in my arms. Taking a bath has never been my thing. Now I'm second guessing that. We slowly wash each other, our soapy hands exploring and caressing every wet inch of our skin.

After our bath, we help each other towel off and go back to bed. Finley and I both hold back laughs as we pick up all the unused condoms.

"Leave one out," I say, as she starts closing my bedside drawer.

"Why?"

"Two words," I reply and then help her onto the bed. "Morning sex."

Her face splits with her smile. "I like the sound of that."

With visions of all of the different ways I can wake her up, I drift off to sleep peacefully.

CHAPTER 17

Finley

AT THIS POINT, Asher is the only Thompson I haven't met. Out of his brothers and sister, I'm closest to Abby. Gideon is a giant flirt and his older brother Eli is a bit cold but Noah said they had a sibling rivalry thing happening and not to take it personally.

From what he's told me about Asher, we have a lot in common. I'm less of a recluse but I can be a homebody and we both work from home. Sure I'm a remote customer service rep for an insurance company and he's a crazy talented woodworker . . . it's close enough.

I pull on my robe and then tug my overnight bag down from the top shelf. "I can be all packed in thirty."

Noah comes up behind me, his hand sliding around my waist as he helps lower my bag to the ground. The body heat from his bare chest warms my back through the material of the robe.

It's insane how much I crave him physically. Two weeks ago we made love for the first time. We haven't been able to keep our hands off of each other since. After we found out Allen left New Hampshire, we started sleeping at my house. Staying at his house delayed the work we were doing on the third floor.

Now that we're back here it makes sense for Noah to sleep over, not that it's work on the house that's been keeping us up late. Last night we got sidetracked when an innocent kiss turned into hours of sex and I already crave him again.

Turning in his arms, I jump and he catches me. My robe is off and lying on the floor by the time we make it to the bed.

Before he climbs over top of me, I roll over to my stomach and rise up onto my hands and knees. "Like this," I plead. "I want you like this."

He presses his hand to my back. "Ask and you shall receive."

I give him a sultry look over my shoulder, catching the heat in his eyes as he stares down at me.

His hand continues to move down my back and over the swell of my ass. He kneads my flesh, the rough feel of his fingers only turning me on more.

I grab a condom from my bedside table and pass it to him. He makes quick work of putting it on before driving into me. My head rears back as I fight the impulse for my arms to buckle.

"Fuck," he groans.

I feel that word all over. There is nothing in the world sexier than the power my body seems to have over him. What's even better, is I feel the same way about his.

We go at each other each morning before work. The hours that we're apart during the day I crave him. When he comes over after work, I practically jump him at the front door. Most of the time we've been able to make it up to my bedroom. The times he laid me out on the dining room table, spread me on the stairs and took me on my kitchen countertop were the only exceptions to that.

His fingers dig into my hips as he pulls me back onto his cock. I fall forward onto the bed and reach my hand between my legs.

"That's it. Touch yourself baby, come all over my dick," he orders.

There's no other sound in the room save the slap of our flesh. He curls his body over mine and turns my face toward him. His lips find mine and he takes my mouth with the same intensity that his body is taking mine.

I cry out my orgasm against his mouth. Not long after, he grunts as he finds his release. When he pulls out he gives my ass a swat. Laughing I wiggle it and both of his hands come down to cup and squeeze my cheeks.

"Face down and ass up, it's like you're trying to kill me," he says, pushing my hip until I topple over to one side.

I watch him as he walks to the bathroom to get rid of the condom. His body was beautiful even before I knew it as well as I do now. Muscular calves that lead to thick thighs and an ass sculpted by a master. His back is nothing to sneeze at either.

If I had to pick a body part I loved the most, other than the one he just pounded me with, it would be his arms. I've never felt more secure anywhere than wrapped tightly in them.

"That doesn't look like packing," Noah jokes as he walks back into the room.

"I don't think I can move," I groan. "You broke me."

He trails his fingertips across the arches of my feet

making me pull away. He chuckles at my reaction. I pout but get ready, mainly because I'm excited about meeting Asher.

It's early December, the roads are clear but it's surreal to see snow on either side of the road. Despite my dad's protests, I have driven in the snow. I haven't gone far and it's been the only times Noah has rode shotgun. He didn't want me to be scared of running to the store or of driving if there was an emergency.

Our drive north is peaceful, a winding two lane highway thick with forests and glimpses of mountain peaks. These are parts of New Hampshire I've never seen before and I'm happy to silently drink in the view with Noah's warm hand resting on my thigh. Two or so hours later, we're turning onto his property.

"That's his house," Noah says pointing out the windshield. "And that's his workshop." Then he nods his head in the direction to a path. "And, the cabin we'll be staying at is down that path."

It's like a Thomas Kinkaid picture come to life. Asher's house is the biggest of the three, an oversized cottage in a snowy fairyland. The workshop is smaller; it's simple architecture blending into instead of distracting from its surroundings. The cabin is the smallest building of the three. That in no way dulls its charm.

"It's beautiful out here," I murmur, opening my door.

"Just wait until you see the lake," Noah replies.

He leaves our bags in his truck and leads me toward the front door.

He knocks on the door but there's no answer. "He's probably in his workshop."

I look over at the direction he's gesturing. "He knows we're coming right?"

He nods his head and shrugs. "Knowing Asher, he's working on something and lost track of time."

As we get closer to the workshop, we hear the sound of a power saw. Since there's no way his brother will hear our knock, Noah pushes open the door.

Asher is facing us, his head down as he cuts a piece of wood. After the wood is cut, he lifts his arm, the saw turning off as he looks up. When he sees us, he tilts to the side before he pulls off his safety glasses.

"Hey bro," he calls.

Asher, who I've only seen in pictures, is proof positive that these Thompsons have amazing genes. His brother is taller than Noah by maybe three inches. Where Noah and Gideon share their mother's coloring, Eli and Asher are dark haired like Mr. Thompson. Noah's hair can get shaggy between cuts but Asher has that whole mountain man thing going on, with his shoulder length dark brown hair and full beard.

To put it mildly, he's seriously hot. As in, off the grid if zombies took over the world you'd want him in your bed—er, by your side—kind of hot.

He sets his safety glasses next to the saw and moves around it to come greet us. Noah pulls him into a hug, patting his back a couple times before letting him go.

"This is Finley," he says, introducing me as I offer Asher my hand.

He takes it, his rough-from-work fingers reminding me of Noah.

"It's nice to finally meet you."

He smiles at me and then turns to Noah. "She's pretty."

Noah drapes his arm around my shoulders, a hint of possessiveness in his movements causing my heart to flutter. "I noticed."

My eyes move around the workshop. It's brilliantly set up. There are large vents above the table saw to pull wood dust from the air, and separate zones for wood carving and staining. There are pieces in various stages of completion around the space. Each one is more stunning than the last.

"You keep working. I'm going to show Finley the cabin."

"I'll come down as soon as I'm done in here," Asher says.

Once we're back outside Noah says, "Don't be offended if we don't see him again until we leave."

I laugh and take his hand. "I've been warned."

As we make our way to the path Noah pointed out earlier, I get my first glimpse of the lake. It roots me where I stand. Noah, not realizing I had stopped, rocks to a halt when he tries to move forward and I don't come.

"It's so beautiful," I sigh.

He squeezes my hand. "I thought you'd like it. Wait until you see the view from the cabin."

That gets me moving. The cabin is simple. It's a log cabin with one main room and a small bathroom. The focal point of it is a large picture window overlooking the lake.

"Wow," I breathe, crossing the room to stand in front of the window.

The lake is small; some would even call it a pond. Its size does nothing to distract from how beautiful it is. If anything it makes it seem all the more magical with its lush circle of snow dusted pine trees surrounding it.

"Can we walk down there?" I ask, pointing to the water.

He offers me his hand. "Let's go."

There are stone steps leading down to the water's edge. Someone, probably Asher, cleared the snow from them. There's a wooden dock to the left of the base of the stairs, below Asher's workshop. There's another set of stone stairs on the other side of Asher's workshop, this one leading to a small beach.

"He has a beach!" I point at the beach and jump up and down excitedly.

Noah laughs and tugs me onto the dock. "We can come back next summer."

"Good. You were right. This place is amazing."

He smiles at me. "I thought you'd like it here."

"You thought right," I reply, and then add, "are you sure we couldn't ice skate on that lake?"

His head jerks with his laugh. "If it's cold enough, maybe in January."

We both sit at the end of the dock and take in the beauty of this place. It's almost too perfect up here. I'm happy to have Noah to share it with. This place, though peaceful, is lonely in a sad way. My thoughts shift to Asher and my heart hurts that he has no one to keep him company here.

"Do you ever worry about your brother?" I ask, changing the subject.

"All the time. I hate that he isolates himself the way he does and feel guilty I don't come up here to check on him that much."

"Does he deliver the pieces he makes?" I ask and Noah shakes his head.

"He does most of his business online and has a delivery service handle the shipping and installation."

"What about food?"

"There's a woman who comes out once a week to clean. She also does his grocery shopping. She even stocked the cabin for us this weekend."

"Does he date?"

He tips his head down to look at me. "Why? Are you interested?"

I elbow him. "I'm curious, not interested. But, I have to say I have about ten friends in Texas that would sleep with him on sight alone."

Noah blinks. "What?"

I grin up at him. "Your brothers are hot. Don't worry though, I think you're the hottest of the bunch."

He growls and gives me a kiss so hot my toes curl. "Don't you forget it."

We sit there for what seems like hours. I pull out my phone to snap pictures for my mom.

It's not until Noah's stomach grumbles and we both want to warm up that we head inside. I stay in the cabin and get a fire going in the woodstove while Noah walks back up to his truck to get our bags. He's faster than I am and starts a late lunch for us after I refuse his help with the fire. I'm a New Englander now; I need to be able to start my own fires.

After I get the fire going and confirm Noah has lunch well under way, I explore the small cabin. "Did your brother make all of this furniture?"

"Not only the furniture, he built his house, the workshop and this cabin."

My mouth drops open. "He did?"

He grins at me. "He had help, but yeah Asher built these."

"That's so cool."

He carries two plates over and we sit on a wood

framed sofa to eat. "It was a big project for him to tackle."

"What did your parents think about him moving up here?"

From what I've seen of his family they are all close and tied to Woodlake.

"The land has been in the family for generations on my mother's side. My uncle inherited it and since he didn't have any kids, he offered it to us before he sold it. The money wasn't important to him but keeping it in the family was.

"He didn't have any kids and was moving to Belize. My parents didn't want it but would have bought it if none of us kids wanted it just to keep someone else from buying it. Asher surprised all of us by not only wanting the land but wanting to build on it.

"He was working for my dad before Eli took over the store and hated it. He's never been comfortable around people and with the way he looks, he got attention he didn't want living in the city."

"Was there anything up here or did he have to build from scratch?"

"Our uncle used to fish up here so there was a shack. It was where this cabin sits now. He lived in that shack while he built his house. I'll never forget the day he finished it. He proved everyone wrong."

"He sure did." I look around, even more impressed now. "So, where are we sleeping tonight?"

One thing I noticed about the cabin was its lack of a bed.

Noah stands and walks over to a cabinet built into one of the cabin walls. He grasps a hook I didn't notice and pulls downward.

"Oh cool," I say as I stand. "It's a murphy bed."

Once Noah has the bed all the way down he lies across it. "Care to join me?"

I cross the room to the door and flip the lock. "Should we close the curtains?"

"And miss out on the view?" Noah counters, tugging off his sweater.

I undress as I close the distance between us. "Will you be looking out the window or at me?"

He pulls me into his arms and kisses me, effectively giving me his answer. For the rest of the weekend we do our best to ignore the view.

CHAPTER 18

Noah

"LET ME GET that." I jump up when I see Finley struggling to carry a box.

We've been home from our weekend away at the cabin for two weeks and things are moving along exactly how I want them to. Well, not exactly. If I'm being honest, I'd rather she just be my wife now.

I love her. Hell, after one weekend with her, even Asher's half in love with her now. Watching her pull him out of his shell was almost magical. She has this way of making people feel comfortable. It must come in handy since she talks to so many people for her job.

"I have it," she argues but doesn't resist my taking it from her.

"Where do you want it?"

She motions to her milk crate coffee table. The crates' days are numbered. We dug out an old steamer trunk out of her shed. It was filthy, but after Finley got it cleaned up, she fell in love with it. She painted it earlier and now, it's drying on a stack of newspaper in her office.

Once I set it down, she pulls a photo album out from the top and motions for me to sit down. She sits next to me and flips it open, gently stroking her hand over the first picture. It's her, on her wedding day.

"God, look at you," I breathe.

I'm jealous of the asshole who was lucky enough to marry her. He should have treasured the gift he was given but instead broke her. He never deserved her. That'll be the regret he has to live with for the rest of his miserable life. There's no way I'll ever make the mistake of not cherishing her.

Her lips tip up in a small smile and she turns the page. There are more pictures, snapshots and not the professional full-length pictures of her. In the first one she's in a robe getting her hair done. The next one is of her with her bridesmaids. Then there's one of her with her flower girl.

"My mom brought this box with her when they came. I wasn't ready to look at these photos then."

She pulls in a breath while I hold mine.

"That's my cousin Heather." She taps the picture with her fingertip.

She turns the page and I see Allen at once.

Her fingertips nervously dance over his photo. "We were so young."

"You need to talk to someone about him."

She gives me a wet laugh, lifting her sleeve to her nose. "But, we're divorced."

I hug her to me. "That doesn't erase your marriage."

She sags against me and I turn the next page for her.

"My dad hated that tie," she mutters, pointing at a photo of her parents. "My mom fussed over it all day."

She sucks in a breath when we get to the picture of

their first kiss as man and wife.

"I was so angry at him for coming here."

"Finley."

She gulps.

I turn the page. "He wasn't the same man you married."

"I know," she agrees, even though her tone doesn't.

Page after page, we flip through her entire album, a single teardrop splashes on the final page.

She hurriedly cleans it away, it's streak blurring the image of them looking out the doorway of a limo, waving goodbye.

I close the album, lean forward to place it on top of the box and then lean back to settle her across my lap.

She cries herself out, eventually falling asleep on me. Once I'm certain I won't wake her, I shift her fully onto the sofa and cover her with a blanket.

Then I carry the box upstairs to one of the spare rooms. I'll tell her if she asks but I don't want her getting upset all over again. Fin has been bottling up all the emotions her ex's visit created. As much as I hate to see her hurting, she's processing years' worth of anger and betrayal. He's lucky he's back in Texas since all I want to do is kick his ass for all the shit he put her through.

I'm on the bottom step when someone knocks on the door. Looking in the direction of the den I race over to it and open it before whoever is on the other side can knock again.

"Hey, Abby," I say, surprised to find my sister there. "What are you doing here?"

She shrugs, stepping past me. "I had an open house not far from here. Where's Finley?"

"She's napping in the den."

Abby takes a step back. "Is it a bad time? I wanted to see the top floor."

She hasn't been by since we finished it and her arrival might be a blessing in disguise. "Now's good. We won't wake her up there."

She steps out of her boots, setting them on a drip tray Finley set up by the door.

"Oh, is that chalk paint?" She asks, pointing to the steamer trunk.

"Yep," I say.

"I like the teal," she whispers.

Then she pulls off her hat and gloves, shoving them into the pockets of her coat before shrugging it off. I take it and drape it over the bottom post of the bannister.

She follows me up the stairs. Some random stuff Finley found in the shed is currently all that's up there.

"Is she still going to move her office up here?" Abby asks, moving to look out one of the dormer windows.

"Not anytime soon." I shake my head. "She's gotten used to having her office downstairs."

"She should get a roommate," Abby says, clearly on a fishing expedition.

I don't take the bait. "Why would she need a roommate?"

Abby gives me a not so innocent shrug. "This big old place and her all by herself."

"You know she's not by herself," I grumble.

"Oh?" She acts surprised. "Are you moving in?"

"Abby," I warn.

"Well, why not? You're in love with her," she argues.

"Now's not a good time." I take a seat in one of the chairs.

She moves quickly to sit across from me. "That doesn't sound good. What happened?"

"She was crying over their wedding album today."

She cringes. "That's awful."

I pinch the bridge of my nose. "I hate seeing her upset."

"It's a good sign she trusts you enough to show her emotions in front of you," Abby says sympathetically.

I drop my hand. "It is?"

She nods. "Can I do anything?"

"I don't know," I admit.

She reaches across the table to grab my hand. "I'm sorry I was being so pushy earlier about you moving in."

I give her hand a squeeze. "It's okay."

"Give her time. It's probably a good thing she looked at those pictures."

"You think?" I ask, wondering if it's a bad thing that I put the box away.

"Of course. Better to cry about it than bottle it all up."

I stand, letting go of her hand. "I need to do something. Wait here. I'll be right back."

With care to not make a racket, I pull the box with the album out of the spare closet and carry it back downstairs. If crying will help her, I'll hold her everyday until she's run out of tears.

Finley hasn't moved an inch from where I settled her. Her eyes are red rimmed from her tears, but she's still the most beautiful woman I've ever seen.

"What did you dash off for?" Abby asks as soon as I'm back.

"Did what I could to avoid a bottle up."

She nods. "She'll get past this, I'm sure of it."

"Thanks Abs." I smile.

A soft smile spreads across her face, reminding me so much of our mother. "Enough about us. Any big deals since the last time we talked?"

She stretches her neck to one side, massaging it with her fingertips. She wrinkles her nose. "It's too cold. Everyone stays inside if they can."

When I frown, she's quick to defend herself. "Oh don't make a face. It happens every year. I'm used to it and have been a good little ant, saving all spring and summer."

"Don't let Gideon hear you calling yourself an ant," I tease.

She crosses her arms. "It's not my fault you're all giants."

"Fair enough, ant," I joke.

Then both of our phones ring.

I pull mine out and furrow my brow. "It's Dad."

Abby holds up her phone. "Eli is calling me."

"That's strange timing." Prickles of unease crawl up the back of my neck as I answer.

"Dad?"

"We're at All Saints. They think mom might have a blood clot," he tells me, his voice coming out in a rush.

I stand as soon as he says All Saints, Woodlake's main hospital. "Abby's with me. We're on the way."

Eli must have given the news to her. With her phone to her ear, she's pale as she follows me. This time I make no effort to silence my steps down the stairs.

"Finley." I shake her shoulder trying to wake her.

She blinks open her eyes. One good look at my face has her quickly sitting upright. "What happened?"

"My mom's at the hospital. I need to go but didn't want you to worry."

She reaches for my hand. "I'm coming with you."

"You've had a rough day." I argue but it's weak. I want her with me but don't want her to feel obligated.

She stands, ignoring my half-hearted protest. "You're not talking me out of this."

When she sees Abby her brows come together in confusion. "Abby?"

"You were asleep when I got here. It's snowing so you'll want a sweater, a warm coat and some boots." Then her eyes move to me. "Give me your keys. I'll start warming up your truck."

"They're on the kitchen counter," I tell her, watching Finley hurry out of the room.

"Let her be there for you." Abby steps close to me, touching my arm, her eyes following the direction of my gaze.

All I can think of is our mom. "Was Eli calling Asher and Gideon?"

"Gideon was the one who called Dad and Eli. I think one of them tried to call Ash but if he's in his workshop there's no telling if he knows or not."

"All set," Finley says, dashing back into the room.

"I still need to warm the truck," Abby says, leaving before I have a chance to ask her anything else.

"What's wrong with your mom?" Finley asks, pulling her purse strap up her arm.

"They said she might have a blood clot." I try to keep my voice strong, but it wavers slightly.

She cringes but doesn't say anything.

When we get to the truck, Abby crawls into the

backseat. She checks her phone a hundred times on the way. Each time letting us know there's no news. As much as I want to tell her to stop, I don't. It's her way of coping. I won't take it away from her.

When we reach the hospital, I drop them at the main entrance. I find I miss Abby's constant updates of no news during the short time it takes me to park.

Gideon meets me at the door.

"Why didn't you call me?" I accuse.

He looks at his feet. "It all happened so fast. I managed one call to the store before they took us back."

His hand shakes and he tries to hide it by shoving it into his pocket. I'm an asshole.

I reach up to squeeze his shoulder and he gives me a nod.

"Now," I start. "Tell me what happened."

He fills me in on our walk from the entrance to the waiting room. Gideon's landscaping business slows to a crawl in the wintertime so he popped in to see her while she had been volunteering at the elementary school Eli's kids go to. The school library recently underwent a remodel, so they were moving around boxes of books. When her leg began swelling, she figured she had pulled a muscle or something.

He has a way of getting what he wants so even though she didn't think there was anything wrong, when he saw how swollen her leg had gotten he talked her into getting it looked at.

"Thank you," I whisper.

He manages to give me half a smile, his way of forgiving me for being pissed earlier.

I take the seat next to Finley, our hands finding each other's before I've finished sitting. Abby sits on the other side of her, talking to Eli.

Gideon paces near the doors that lead to the treatment rooms. Every time they open we all look.

"She's going to be okay," Finley promises.

The seats are uncomfortable and don't have adjustable arms like at the movie theater. If they did, I'd push it up and pull her close.

"I feel silly now for being so upset earlier."

Not caring about our audience I cup her face in my hands. "I love you."

Her already puffy red eyes refill with tears. "You do?"

Her words are barely audible but I hear her all the same.

"I do," I affirm.

She presses her lips together, one tear spilling down her cheek.

"I think I've loved you since you talked me into letting you help with the house," she whispers.

"I win. I've loved you since you sneezed on me."

A burst of laughter escapes her and then with wide eyes she covers her mouth in embarrassment.

"Life doesn't run on a schedule. We get the bad right along with the good. So today started off bad. You're going through things but I'm here to help you and my mom might have a blood clot, which is scary, but her being here in this hospital means they can help her. You just told me you loved me. Right now I can handle the bad stuff because you're all the good I'll ever need."

Finley stares at me, her lips parted.

Before either she or I can say anything, Abby loudly informs the entire waiting room that Asher is on the way.

"See?" I say, cocking my head in her direction. "Now we have a miracle seeing as how my brother listened to a voicemail the same day he got it."

Her lips tip up into a sweet smile and I give her a soft kiss. After I settle myself back into my chair she leans over the armrest to lay her head against my shoulder.

Abby watches us with a sly smile on her face. She doesn't hide she heard us and knowing my match making little sister, she's loving every second of it.

Asher arrives not long after, making me mentally question how fast he drove. As if waiting for all of us to be together, our father appears like a rabbit pulled from a magician's hat.

We all stand, circling around him in a family huddle. "It's a clot. It's in her thigh. They've admitted her and started her on a blood thinner but she needs to stay the night."

"Can we see her?" Abby asks, her question followed by grunts of agreement from my brothers.

"Yes, but only if you all promise not to excite her. She needs her rest."

I saw him earlier in the week. Tonight, he looks ten years older. It could be the harsh overhead lights, but his skin looks ashen.

I give his arm a squeeze. "Okay Dad."

"Two at a time," he says. "Abby and Gideon, you two go in and see her first."

Eli opens his mouth but quickly snaps it shut after a warning look from our dad. I can't tell if he's on edge because Brooke isn't here. It's late so it makes sense that she wouldn't want the kids up all night in a hospital. Still, I don't know if that's an excuse or not, or if she's still staying at her sister's. Eli's sure as shit not about to share.

Abby looks at Eli, Asher and me. "We won't take too long."

"You're a good girl," Dad mutters, patting her back and then says, "There's a waiting area closer to her new room. Follow me."

Her room is two floors up and down a long hall. The waiting room is half the size of the one in the emergency room but empty and has a loveseat.

I claim that one for Finley and me. Without the armrest between us, we're both more comfortable. Asher comes to sit on the other side of her.

"Hey Finley," he greets her.

She smiles at him. During our stay at his cabin she won him over.

"Stop flirting with my girl," I grumble giving him a grin.

"Then you shouldn't have picked such a pretty one." He grins.

Eli paces in front of us, his phone to his ear. He's talking to Brooke but whatever he says I can't hear.

"Eli, you and Asher are up," Abby says, coming into the waiting room.

"Where's Dad?" Asher asks, standing.

It's Gideon who answers. "They're setting up a cot for him. He's staying the night with Mom."

Eli ends his call and shoves his phone into his pocket before looking at Asher. "Let's go."

As soon as they're gone I turn to Abby. "How is she?"

She frowns. "Her leg looks awful but you know Mom. They're going to need to strap her down to keep her in that bed."

I grin. That sounds like our mom.

Abby leans forward to give me a hug. "I'm not sure why I'm so exhausted. All we did was sit around."

Finley rubs her back as Abby smiles sleepily at her.

I squeeze my little sister tight before looking at Gideon. "Give her a ride home and see her inside."

He nods, putting his hand on her shoulder and turning her from my arms and into his.

"I'll call you later," Abby says to Finley before Gideon leads her away.

As soon as they're gone, Finley and I reclaim our loveseat.

"How are you really?" She asks, her face upturned toward me.

Since we're alone I tell her the truth. I blow out a breath. "Until Dad came out I was worried."

"I would be, too, if it was my mom. I never thought about what would happen if either one of them had to go to the hospital now that I'm so far away."

"Do you ever think of moving back?" I ask her, a little worried at what her answer could be.

With every task we complete on her house I wonder if we're one step closer to her leaving me when it's all done.

"No," she replies forcefully.

"You haven't lived through a full winter yet," I tease.

"You'll keep me warm," she teases back, squeezing her arms around me.

I kiss her temple. "I sure will."

It's not long before Asher and Eli return. "Mom's ready for you."

I stand, pulling up Finley with me. She freezes when I

point both of us in the direction of her room.

"Oh, I'll wait here," she says.

"Nope." I give her hand a little tug. "You're coming with."

Her eyes go wide. "Your mom wants to see you, not me."

"Go on with him," Asher says. "He's too stubborn to fight. Trust me, I know and mom asked to see you."

Finley pulls in a breath. "In that case."

I take her hand and lift it to my lips. My dad's cot is set up on the far side of the room. He gives us a wave as we walk in.

The room is dim, only the light above her bed and the glow from the TV are on.

Even though I've been taller than her since tenth grade, she's always been larger than life to me. It's a shock to see how small she looks in her hospital bed.

"You're so sweet to come," my mom ignores me and greets Finley.

"I'm so sorry to hear you aren't feeling well. I hope the medicine works quickly." She leans down, lightly squeezing my mom's forearm.

I lean over her bed to kiss her cheek. Her hand comes up to pat my face as I do.

"Love you Mom."

"Love you my sweet boy," she whispers back.

CHAPTER 19

Finley

"**T**HIS IS SILLY," Daisy grumbles.

"Would you rather spend another day in the office of the store?" Noah counters.

She looks away which is answer enough for Noah.

"You're doing me a favor," I put in. "It gets so boring during the day."

She frowns but manages to do it sweetly, which is a skill. "You're only saying that."

I sit down next to her. "I'm not."

She looks back at Noah. "You all worry too much."

He smiles down at her. "Wonder where we got that from?"

She smirks but doesn't argue. Noah motions for me to follow him. Before I get up, I pat her arm. After she gives me a small smile I stand up and move to where Noah is waiting for me.

"Don't let her guilt trip you." Noah pulls me close.

"She's not going to guilt trip me," I argue.

He gives me a look and I don't tell him that guilt trip only really works on direct family members.

"Thank you for letting her stay with you," he says, kissing my forehead.

"It's no trouble." I tilt my chin up so he'll kiss my lips instead.

He takes the hint and drops his lips to mine. I hope this feeling never goes away. That's the part that's scaring me the most about my relationship with Noah. People change. Allen did.

I'm not sure I could recover if Noah ever did. As much as I love him, and I do, I'm still holding a piece of my heart back from him.

"Go get some work done," I order.

He kisses me again before saying, "Call me if she gives you any trouble."

His mother was released from the hospital two days ago. After she was admitted, the doctor determined the blood thinner was not taking care of the blood clot as they had hoped it would.

They did a procedure to break it up. The blood thinner worked a bit too well afterward and she had issues bleeding. While they straightened out the dosage, she remained in the hospital. She was there a week, Mr. Thompson slept in her room each night.

She went home after her release and promptly told Mr. Thompson he'd make her a murderer and a widow if he didn't stop hovering. He believed her enough to try and bring her to the store with him the next day.

There, both Mr. Thompson and her oldest fussed over her. She refused to go back which is why she's here with me today. Technically, she's well enough to be home by herself but it seems to be a Thompson trait to worry.

Since I work from home, I offered to let her hang out with me.

She can camp out on the sofa and watch TV or nap while I work. The kitchen and bathroom are close to the den. She's supposed to move around a bit but not do any stairs.

I watch him from the door, waving as he pulls away. Closing the door once he's out of sight, I lean my back against it and pull in a breath. Allen's mom never liked me. Mrs. Thompson, or Daisy as she's told me to call her, seems to like me but that's how Allen's mom was in the beginning too.

"You can do this," I murmur to myself.

Stepping into my office I log into my work computer. It's on the slow side so I like to putter around in the morning while it gets going. It's a laptop so I can work from the den.

"Up for company?" I ask. "I don't want you to think I'm fussing but I was thinking about working in here today if that's okay with you."

She smiles. "Of course I'd love your company. It'll give me a chance to get to know you better."

"I'm boring," I admit.

She shakes her head. "That's not what Noah thinks."

My cheeks redden as I wonder what he's told his mother about me. "He's wonderful."

She smiles outright. "I'm happy you think that."

I motion to the kitchen. "Can I get you anything to eat, to drink?"

She shakes her head and I say, "I'm going to grab my computer. I'll be right back."

My boss knows Daisy is with me so I'm off of phone duty today so I leave my headset on my desk.

The steamer trunk I cleaned and painted is a much better resting place for my laptop than the old crates I used before.

"So, what would you like to do today?"

She tilts her head to the side and I know instantly that's where Noah picked that up. "I'd like to know more about you."

I fight back a cringe but must not do a good job of it when she laughs, "I'm not going to bite."

"I'm sorry," I giggle. "I feel like I'm fifteen again meeting my first boyfriend's parents."

"Were they awful?" She inquires. "Leave you scarred for life?"

I shake my head. "No, they were great."

She lifts her chin. "See, nothing to worry about."

She has a point. "What would you like to know?"

Leaning closer to me, she gives my knee a squeeze. "Everything."

"Oh geez," I laugh. "If you wanted to take a nap you could have just said so."

She grins. "Don't be silly."

"Well, where should I start?" I ask.

"Noah said that before you moved here, you had never worked on a house before. What gave you the courage to tackle this house?"

Before his dad dropped off his mom, Noah started a fire in the den. My eyes dance around the room. I live here, I work here, and some days it still feels like a dream.

"My marriage wasn't a happy one but the divorce still rocked me. I didn't know which way was up. One day I watched this show. You may have seen it. It's a husband

and wife from Texas who transform houses."

"Shiplap," she exclaims, making me laugh.

"Yes, they sure love installing or uncovering those wooden planks on walls," I agree.

"It's a great show. The houses they fix up always look so pretty in the reveal," she murmurs.

I nod. "I needed to escape the reality of what I thought was going to be my unhappily ever after. That show struck a cord deep within me. I felt like I was living in the before and if I could fix up a house I could fix up myself along the way."

Her eyes move over my face, assessing me before she asks. "Did it work?"

For some reason her question makes me want to cry. I suck in a breath.

"I think the house is now in better shape than I am."

"Noah told me you've been a bit blue," she confesses.

One thing I like about Noah is the fact that he's close with his family. I remind myself of this to stop from worrying what his mom thinks of me for crying over my ex the way I did.

My nose starts stinging and I get up to grab a tissue. "I'm sorry. I don't know why I'm crying."

When I sit back down she pats my knee. "I'd be more concerned if you weren't."

I gulp and dab at the corners of my eyes. "But we're divorced."

She shrugs. "A divorce does not erase a marriage. You were so focused on all this work you've done you weren't able to mourn its end. Now you are."

I nod.

She gives me a gentle smile. "Give yourself time."

"I will," I promise.

Changing the subject so I can work and not spend the day crying in front of Noah's mom, I ask, "I'm sure I can find the house show on demand, would you like to watch some?"

She agrees and I get the show going. Deciding to make a plate of food for both of us, I head to the kitchen. I figure this way if she's hungry she doesn't need to ask if it's already within arm's reach.

She likes coffee so I refill my mug and pour another for her. Once I've got the spread laid out, I focus on getting some work done.

Every so often, I sneak a glance at the food, pleased when I notice a muffin missing.

I try not to baby her each time she gets up. She's supposed to be taking it easy but she isn't on full bed rest. It's important for her to be moving around.

Knowing this doesn't stop me from worrying she'll fall or have some sort of relapse while I'm supposed to be keeping an eye on her.

"I think this one is my favorite so far," she says.

"Oh yeah?" I ask. "What part do you like best?"

"The built in with all the mugs. I might ask Asher to make one of those for me."

"I love the giant mantels. Someday I want to do something to these."

My eyes move around the room. "Noah showed you pictures, right? Of what this house looked like before he helped me renovate it?"

She nods. "We questioned his sanity at first, until Abby mentioned how he couldn't take his eyes off you."

For some reason that has me blushing while I mentally kick myself for not catching on. "Even after months and months of work, this place is still such a blank slate. I have floors, walls, plumbing that doesn't leak, appliances, and furniture. Every time I start to think about changing paint colors or hanging pictures on the wall my mind goes blank."

"There's no rush dear," Daisy replies. "When Noah's dad and I were first starting out, we didn't have much. Over time, as pieces caught our eye, we decorated."

"You don't think it looks bad do you?" I press. "All these empty walls?"

She shakes her head. "Absolutely not."

We start another episode. Her eyes are on the screen. From the corner of mine, I watch her, liking her more and more.

Before she catches me staring at her, I get back to work.

"Hello," Noah calls, surprising both of us as he comes in through the kitchen door.

"Hey," I reply, smiling broadly at him.

"Are you checking up on me?" Daisy accuses.

"Yes I am," he admits with a smile and then lifts a bag. "And I brought lunch."

Her eyes move to the bag. "It smells good. What is it?"

His brows go up. "First, am I forgiven?"

She smirks but after a moment nods.

"I picked up your favorite soup and turkey bacon sandwiches from that place on Fifth Street."

Her eyes drift closed as she inhales. "You're too good to me."

"You can admit it. I'm your favorite," he replies.

She waves her hand at him and she shakes her head.

I stand. "Leave her alone and help me serve."

As soon as we're in the kitchen and out of eyesight of his mother, he sets the takeout bags on the counter and leans down to press his lips to mine.

"That's better," he murmurs after thoroughly kissing me.

"Stop mauling her so we can eat," his mom jokes from the den.

I laugh, pressing my face to his chest.

"I'm not mauling her," Noah argues.

She makes a noise of disagreement but doesn't argue further.

"How's she been?" Noah asks as we plate the food he brought.

"She's been great. We're having a TV marathon."

"I can't thank you enough for letting her hang out here."

"It's no trouble," I say. "She's great company."

His head tilts to the side in the way his mother did earlier. "Have you been lonely here during the day?"

I can't lie to him. "Not all the time."

He kisses me again. "We can't have that."

I smile up at him. "You already have enough to worry about."

He shrugs. "We've already established the fact that I love you, right?"

Unable to dispute that, I nod my head.

"It means I'm going to worry about you no matter what," he explains.

"Can we talk about it more later?" I ask, remembering his mom is not only within ear's reach but waiting for her lunch.

After we eat, once Daisy is back in the den watching

another home makeover, Noah pulls me upstairs.

"Your mom is in the house," I warn, not sure why we need to have our conversation in my bedroom.

He closes the door behind us. "I know."

"Noah," I plead.

He grins at me. "I'm not going to do anything."

My nerves begin to relax and he keeps talking. "I wanted to check on you where you wouldn't worry if she could hear you."

"Oh," I say, surprised. "You didn't have to. Honestly, she's been sweet. All we've done is watch TV."

His eyes hold mine. "We should probably get back downstairs before she tries to sneak clean your kitchen."

"My kitchen is clean," I argue.

"Then she'll rearrange your spices."

"Why on earth would she do that?" I ask.

He laughs, leaning down to kiss me so his laughter ends against my lips.

When he's done kissing me, he says, "We've never been able to figure out why."

He opens the door for me and holds my hand as we make our way back downstairs. At the mouth of the den I look left, expecting to see her on my sectional.

She isn't there.

"Daisy?"

"In here," she murmurs from the kitchen.

I look right and watch as she closes the cabinet door below my sink.

Noah shakes with restrained laughter next to me. "Were you looking for something?"

She dusts her hands and mutters something

unintelligible as she moves past us and back into the den.

"Did she move anything around?" Noah asks as I cross the kitchen to look under my sink.

"She did," I quietly laugh, pointing to the box of trashcan liners.

His head turns in the direction of the den. "I should have warned you."

"I don't mind." I laugh.

Ignoring the fact that his mom is in the next room, Noah pushes me against the counter and kisses me hard. I coil my arms around his neck and hold on, letting him overwhelm me.

"Now go, so I can get my work done and so you don't embarrass me in front of your mom," I order, after coming up for air.

"We're finishing what we started later," he promises.

I feel a full body tingle at his words, my eyes moving to the time display on my microwave. His gaze follows mine and when he sees what I'm looking at he gives me a wicked grin.

"I need to say bye to my mom before I go or she'll have my head," he says, turning me toward the den.

I can't argue since my mom is the same way.

She pauses the show when we walk in, using the remote I showed her. Noah leans down to kiss her cheek.

"Is dad picking you up later?"

She nods. "I think so."

"Have you talked about what you're doing tomorrow?"

Her eyes move to mine. "I think I'll be fine at home tomorrow."

"How about you and dad talk it out and let us know

tonight?"

"You're welcome here anytime," I add, meaning it.

He squeezes my hand in a silent thanks.

"I'll sort it out with your father," she agrees, and then smiles at me before saying, "I have enjoyed getting to know you better."

Noah drops my hand to wrap his arm around my shoulders, tucking me close. "I knew you would."

She shakes her head. "Now you get back to work so Finley and I can get back to our show."

He turns, looking at the paused TV. "I know this show. You don't know how many clients ask for shiplap after watching it."

Daisy and I look at each other and burst out laughing.

"What did I say?" Noah asks, confused.

"Inside joke," I laugh, moving to my spot on the couch.

His eyes move from his mom to me and back to his mom before saying, "I'm not even going to ask."

"Good idea," I joke.

"Either of you need a fresh drink or anything before I go?"

We shake our heads. "No thanks."

I watch him go, noticing how the room dims as soon as he's gone.

"I like this."

"The show?" I ask, not sure what she's talking about the show or how Noah and I are together.

She shakes her head. "You look at my Noah the way I looked at his father in the beginning."

I gulp, not sure how to respond.

"You're a sweet girl for keeping me company today.

It's been a long time since Noah showed any interest in a woman. It seems he was waiting for one who would be worth his time."

Wow.

"He's great," I start but she cuts me off.

"And he has excellent taste."

That has my cheeks reddening but I hold her gaze.

"Now, let's see how these two transform this house," she says, changing the subject and unpausing the TV.

I'm grateful for it, grateful for everything actually, her words and now the relief I feel from hearing them. It's as if by turning our attention back to the show she's given me the privacy to mull over what she said.

We lapse into a companionable silence, the show and the taps of my fingertips against my keyboard the only noise. She seems focused on the show while I'm less so.

My thoughts are only partly on the work I'm doing as well, luckily it's just electronic claims filings, the busy non-phone related work I could do in my sleep at this point.

No, my thoughts are on Noah and on my own fears at what our future holds.

CHAPTER 20

Noah

"JUST ASK HER," Abby orders.

I stare at her and then raise my brows.

She frowns and replies. "Well, why the hell not?"

Things between Finley and I were going great and then life happened. Mom getting hospitalized, even though she's fine now, was a shock. Other than needing to be on a blood thinner for the next six months or so, things have gone back to normal for her.

She spent a few days hanging out at Finley's place right after she was discharged, mainly so she wouldn't kill my dad for hovering over her. Finley took my mom staying with her in stride. In fact, they were cackling like old girlfriends by the second day and now when my mom wants to get a hold of me, she calls Finley.

Then, to save money, Fin decided against spending Christmas with her parents in Texas. She wasn't homesick but she couldn't hide how much she missed her family. The look on her face when her parents, aunts, uncles and cousin showed up to surprise her was priceless.

She went from shock to happy and then to panic at trying to figure out where everyone would sleep in less than a minute. Together, we figured out temporary sleeping arrangements for everyone and the rest of their visit went off without a hitch. It was plain to see how much getting to spend the holidays with her family meant to her.

That was a month ago, a month of me sleeping here each and every night. A month of swinging by my house every day to drop off the trailer if I had it; and to repack my overnight bag. We're close, closer than ever but there's this wall I can't break through.

"It's not like I can ask her to move in with me. She loves that house and isn't going to leave it."

"Call it something else. Say you want to take things to the next level and see if she gets the hint and asks you to move in with her."

I lean back into my chair and look up at the ceiling. "Last thing I want to do is pressure her if she isn't ready."

"You've never been one to beat around the bush, Noah. Why don't you tell her what you're feeling?" She asks.

I tip my head back to meet her eyes. "Would you believe me if I said I'm scared she doesn't feel the same?"

Abby's eyes bug out. "Don't be insane. She loves you."

Her words should ease my concerns but they don't. I can't imagine my life without her. I'm impatient for it to begin. I want it all, marriage, a family, and to grow old together.

She's still struggling with so much. All I can do is wait even though it's the last thing I want to do.

"Want me to drop a hint?" She asks after a bit.

"What kind of hint?" I counter.

"I can play dumb and ask when you're moving in for good or if you've put your house on the market yet, something like that," she answers.

I have to admit, it's not a bad idea. "Do you think that would work?"

She shrugs but does it with a catlike grin. "Have I ever failed?"

I grin back and she stands. "You call Jon and meet him for a drink. Knowing you and how quickly you've been dashing home after work each day, it's probably been ages since you've gone to happy hour."

"It has been a while," I admit.

"Call Finley and tell her I'm swinging by for a visit and that you'll be late," she tells me, still ordering me around.

It's my turn to stand, pulling my phone from my pocket as we walk together from my office to the main door, waving at Justin as we pass him.

"Hey baby," I greet when she answers.

"Everything okay?"

She's not used to me calling after work, normally after popping by my house, I head right to hers.

"I'm going to be late tonight if that's alright."

"Oh," she hesitates before saying, "of course."

"Abby stopped by here and plans to head your way. If you don't want company let me know and I'll tell her another night."

"Don't be silly. I'd love to see her," she says, her voice lighter than moments before.

I smile at Abby and lift my head. "She'll be there in a few then."

She doesn't reply and I pull my phone from my ear to

make sure I didn't drop the call. When I see I haven't, I ask, "Finley?"

"Where are you going?" Her question is whispered; so quiet I need to strain to hear her.

"I'm going to meet Jon for a drink," I reply.

"Jon?" There's a relief in her tone.

"Want me to ask him if Em and him can come over for dinner sometime next week?"

"I'd like that." The worry from her voice is now gone.

"Consider it done," I promise. "And, I won't stay out too long, just a drink."

"Don't worry, Abby will keep me company."

"Alright baby" I answer. "I love you."

"I love you too Noah."

After I hang up with her I give Abby a hug goodbye.

"I'll call you and let you know what she says," Abby shouts as she walks away.

Staying in front of our office, I wave as she pulls away and then I call Jon. "Feel like a drink?"

"Trouble in paradise?"

"The opposite," I reply.

"Why aren't you heading to Finley's?" He asks, surprise coloring his words even through the phone.

"I'll tell you over a drink, unless tonight isn't good for you?" I ask belatedly.

"Tonight is perfect. I was on my way to an empty house and leftovers."

"Where's Emily?" I ask, moving toward my truck.

"Some book club but they should call it a wine club because all they do is drink and gossip from what I hear."

"Jesus," I laugh, picturing Emily drunk.

"Tell me about it," he laughs.

As I start my truck I reply, "I'll see you in five and you can."

I beat him there and order a drink for each of us.

"Hey man," he greets, sitting on the stool next to mine when he shows up.

"Thanks for meeting me," I say, pushing his drink toward him.

"Always got time for you man," he answers, before taking a drink.

"That means a lot to me."

"So, are you going to ask Finley to marry you?" He asks, surprising me.

"Someday, I hope. Right now I'd be happy with moving in together," I admit.

"You thinking about selling your place?"

I shrug, and then lean forward against the bar, my hands circling my glass. "I'm not attached to it the way Finley is to her place."

"So why are you here drinking with me and not there with her?" He asks.

"I'm too chickenshit to ask her how she feels so Abby's over there right now doing it for me," I laugh.

He rubs my back as he laughs with me. "Fucking Abby. That girl is a riot," he wheezes.

I hold up my glass in a cheer. "Here's to hoping Finley wants to live with me too."

"She will," he replies, touching his glass to mine. "I'm sure of it."

"That makes one of us," I joke.

Truth is, tension coils from my gut outward to each of my limbs. Before Jon got here, I was staring at my phone like a teenager. Even now, I want to check it which is crazy because I know my ringer is on.

"Want to come over for dinner next week?" I ask.

He nods. "She's a damn fine cook. I'll have to check with Em on the day but I'll say yes anyway."

"You tell me the day, we'll make it happen." I assure him.

We finish our drink, and then another before Abby calls.

Jon takes one look at me and says, "Fill me in tomorrow."

I give him a grateful nod, slip some bills across the bar top before answering her call. "How'd it go?"

"I asked her when you were moving in and she dropped a plate, breaking it."

"That doesn't sound good," I mutter, pushing open the door of the bar. "What happened after?"

"She said you two haven't discussed anything like that."

I inhale, pressing the button to unlock my truck.

"I asked her why not," Abby rushes on.

"And?" I ask, when she doesn't say anything else.

"I think she's waiting for you to bring it up," she tells me.

"And if I do, you think she'd say yes?" I ask, crossing my fingers and toes and anything else.

"I do," she admits.

With a grin I gaze out my windshield. "I better go then."

"Good luck bro, not that you'll need it," she teases.

Every light between the bar and her house is green. By the last light, the one closest to her neighborhood, I feel the weight of all my hopes pushing me along.

The lights of her house greet me. She's in there, waiting for me.

"Still up?" I shout, after letting myself in the front door.

I shrug off my coat and toe off my boots.

"I'm in the kitchen!" she calls back.

I lock up and then move toward her only to find her leaning against the end of the hall before the entry to the kitchen and den.

"God, you're beautiful," I say as soon as I'm close enough to reach her.

"Shh," she replies, not fighting me as I pull her into my arms.

I kiss her, planning for it to be a simple hello. It becomes something entirely different and seconds later I have her pressed up against the wall, our bodies colliding with intense need.

She pulls at my clothes, I tear at hers. A month after our relationship went physical, she went on birth control. It's given us the freedom to be spontaneous. This feels like something else, something more.

"I'll never stop wanting you," I groan, my hands moving over her, trying in vain to touch all of her.

"Noah," she cries, clutching me as she comes undone.

I follow her, spiraling down after her.

Still breathing heavily, we stare at each other.

I push her hair back from her face and grin at her. "Hello."

She bursts out laughing and tucks her face into my neck. Scooping her up, I carry her into the den, careful not to trip with my pants halfway around my ankles.

I set her on the sofa and rearrange my clothes, watching as she straightens hers. As soon as we're both fully dressed, I kiss her again, this time the gentle hello I originally intended.

When I pull back I say the words that have been eating away at me. "I don't want to live out of an overnight bag any longer. I want to live with you Finley."

"Yes."

"Yes, you want that too?" I confirm.

She presses her lips together and nods.

"I want to sell my place," I tell her, raising my eyebrows.

"I know a realtor," she says without hesitation, biting her lip.

We both grin at each other and I kiss her, pushing her onto her back on the couch as I do.

Lifting my head, I gaze down at her. "I'm paying for the new windows."

She blinks at me and then asks, "What?"

"And I'm building you a garage," I add.

Her arms coil around my neck. "Is this your idea of pillow talk?"

"And the roof," I answer before kissing her.

She giggles throughout and I've never been happier.

"When do you want to move in?"

"Is tonight too soon?"

God, her smile, one look at it and I feel invincible.

"How should we celebrate?" I ask, kissing her neck.

"I have a feeling we already did," she jokes.

She'll learn I've barely started our celebrations.

"And a hot tub," I say.

She blinks. "A hot tub?"

"Yep, after I put in a back patio," I say.

She shakes her head. "You're crazy."

"But before all of that, I'm buying you a ring," I murmur.

She goes stock-still.

"Fin?"

She doesn't reply.

"Finley, say something," I plead.

"Do you mean a wedding ring?" She asks, her voice a whisper.

"I do," I confirm.

"Really?"

Sliding my hand up into her hair, I pull her lips down to mine. "I've never been surer of anything."

We kiss and she melts into me, trusting me, believing me, knowing that I'd never lie to her.

When I lift my head, breaking our kiss, she wipes tears from her eyes.

"I love you," she murmurs.

"So you'll wear my ring?" I confirm.

With her lips pressed together, looking like she's holding back a fresh wave of tears, she nods.

"I love you so much Fin," I murmur, kissing her temple. "And, I'm only catching up. I've watched you work so hard to transform this place. You have me now."

She reaches up to cup my cheek, her eyes wet. "I've had you from the start, from day one."

"And you always will," I promise.

Her face goes soft, dreamy like. "I believe you."

"You better."

Then she giggles. "A hot tub?"

It's my turn to laugh. "Damn straight."

Sitting back, I pull her up with me.

"You wait here," she says. "I have something I think you'll like."

She returns, this time with a plate. I missed dinner, and she had made my favorite.

Taking the plate from her, I set it on the steamer trunk. "Did you eat?"

"I did, with Abby," she replies.

"I'm lucky she didn't eat it all," I joke.

She sits next to me, retrieving my plate and setting it on my lap. "Now eat."

"How soon will you list it?" My mom asks.

"Abby's here with me now, taking pictures. Then I'm heading home to Fin," I reply.

"We love Finley for you Noah. She's a great girl."

"The best," I correct her.

"You waited for the right one."

"I did." I nod my head, even though she can't see me.

"When can we come over?"

"Give us the weekend for me to unpack," I plead, hopeful that she isn't already on her way to Finley's.

"I suppose," she mutters.

I catch Abby's eye and say, "Thanks Mom."

Abby waits nearby and watches as I hang up.

"Any bets on whether she'll give you the weekend before she descends?" She asks as I slip my phone into my back pocket.

"I'm not taking that bet," I mutter. "How long do you think it will take to sell?"

She frowns. "Sales slow down during the winter months but with that garage and how well the place will show, I'd be shocked if it doesn't sell fast."

That's great news, I think to myself.

Our conversation on splitting things was frustrating. She seems to think putting the windows and a garage in is too much. I haven't told her I'm going to replace the siding yet. I figured it'd be better to ask for forgiveness than permission.

"I'm all done here. I'll have the listing up by morning," Abby replies.

We walk out together. She's blocked me in so I sit in my truck and wait, watching until my path is clear.

This place is empty now. We didn't need to hire movers. Between Jon and my trucks and the trailers, it only took a couple of trips to get all of my things to Finley's.

We're putting my bedroom set in the master since it's nicer. Her TV is going there and, since mine is bigger it's going in the living room. Her bed is going in one spare room and my spare set is in the other.

She has enough kitchen things to serve a battalion so Gideon took mine. We split my living room set between her office and the third floor.

Fin was hanging up my clothes in our closet when I left. I told her to leave it. Each shirt she pulled from a box she stroked with gentle care. With one of my shirts still in her hands, I wrapped my arms around her middle and held her back to my front. She leaned back into me, holding my arms to her with one hand and lifting the hanger to the rod with the other.

I kissed the top of her head and left her to it. When I get back to the house only the kitchen light is on downstairs. I go straight upstairs and find Finley working in one of the spare rooms.

"You could have waited for me to help," I greet.

She lowers her hammer. "I wanted to surprise you."

"You like them?" I ask, nodding my head toward the black and white prints.

They're hockey themed close-ups. One is an extreme close-up of a puck, its shadow gray against the ice. Another one is hovering at an angle over what would be the blue line if the print were color. There's one of the sharpened blades of a pair of skates and the last one of the goal net.

"I know nothing about hockey but they look cool," she says, her eyes taking them in.

"Nothing about hockey," I grumble making her giggle.

"I'll take you to a game someday," I promise.

Her brows come together. "Could we watch one here?"

I cross the room and help her hang the last print. "In bed."

She swats at my stomach. "How do you manage to make watching a hockey game sound dirty?"

"It can be the first thing we watch in bed." I grin waggling my brows.

"Right now?" She laughs. "Is there even a game on tonight?"

I doubt she has a hockey package on her cable plan. That's another thing that will be changing.

"Let's call it a night and see what we can find?" I suggest.

She looks around the room, her eyes round. "There's still so much to put away."

"It'll all still be there tomorrow," I counter.

Her drive and focus are one of the things I love most about her. She has this inner strength that won't quit, it's what led her to coming here. That doesn't mean she doesn't overdo it.

"Tonight we're going to bed early," I say, my tone non-negotiable.

She stops looking around at the boxes we'll still need to unpack and focuses all of her attention on me. "Are you tired?"

I dip my head and kiss her, lifting her as I do.

When I break our kiss to gaze down at her I mutter, "Not tired."

She wraps her arms around my neck and smiles. "I can see that."

I set her down and turn her toward the door. With my hands on her shoulders I follow her to our room.

"Will we need snacks and drinks?" She asks. "If you want, we can make a picnic of it."

Once we're in our room I spin her to face me and kiss her again. She looks adorably confused when I lift my head and start walking her backward to the bed.

As she lies back on it, I pull my shirt off. Leaning over her, I make quick work of undoing the buttons of her flannel shirt. Opening it, I lower my lips to the swell of her breasts.

"This is an interesting introduction to hockey," she sighs, her fingers threading into my hair.

CHAPTER 21

Finley

NOAH OFFICIALLY MOVED in two months ago, and the new roof, siding, and windows are already done. No more worn gray exterior and sad roof. Now crisp white vinyl wraps our home, new black shutters framing the new windows, and charcoal shingles top it off.

"It's done," I say, my voice wavering.

"Why do you sound like you're going to cry babe?" Noah asks, tugging me closer.

We're standing on the street in front of our house. Before Noah moved in, he said there were some things he was going to do as his way of investing in the house since there's no mortgage for him to chip in on.

He wasn't lying.

I never thought he was, I just didn't expect for him to jump on these projects the way he did.

"It's done and now it's like I have no idea what to do next," I reply.

He tips his face down to stare into my eyes. "It's not

done."

"What?" I ask, confused.

"It's not done," he repeats, this time more firmly.

Lifting my arm I make a sweeping gesture towards the house. "What are you talking about?"

"It's going to grow with us so it will never be done." His ocean blue eyes are still on mine.

I never thought about it like that, still I ask, "It will?"

Shifting from beside me to behind me, he wraps his arms around my middle and bends to rest his chin on my shoulder.

One of his arms comes up as he points toward the spare bedrooms on the second floors. "We're going to fill those rooms with babies."

My heart starts to hammer wildly in my chest. "Yes?"

He pulls his arm back to hug me even closer to him. "We may even need to build an addition for all of them."

"An addition?" I breathe.

"Yep," he says, kissing the spot below my ear. "But, before that, you have a wedding to plan."

"So we're not done at all," I murmur.

"No, we're only getting started," he promises, his breath hot on my neck. Then he moves in front of me, facing me with an open jewelry box in his a hand, a gorgeous diamond winking from its velvet bed. Plucking that perfect ring from its perch he tosses the box over his shoulder with a grin. I'm laughing as he takes my hand.

Holding the ring up to the end the fourth finger of my left hand, he smiles at me, a smile I've never seen before. It's nervous and excited at the same time. "Let's start with this," his voice wavers slightly before sliding it on.

He gives me no time to admire it, or answer his

unasked question, sweeping me into his arms and kissing me thoroughly. Lifting my hand behind his head, I peek at it, and am not the least bit surprised to see it's a perfect fit.

THE END

ALSO BY
Carey Heywood

The Him & Her Series
Him
Her
Them
Sawyer Says (Spin off)
Being Neighborly (Spin off)

The Carolina Days Series
The Other Side of Someday (Courtney & Clay)
Yesterday's Half Truths (Lindsay & Luke)
Chasing Daylight (McKenzie & Mitch)

The Love Riddles Series
Why Now? (Kacey & Jake)
Why Lie? (Sydney & Heath)
Why Not? (Reilly & Trip)

Standalones
Better
Stages of Grace
Uninvolved
A Bridge of Her Own

ACKNOWLEDGMENTS

This book was inspired by my love of all things home improvement. I've spent many hours binge watching folks on TV hunt for houses to buy, and then transform them. Those shows have inspired my husband and I to tackle project after project on our own fixer upper home.

For never backing away from a challenge, I'd like to thank my husband Seth. He is my best friend and has my back as he encourages me to chase after my dreams.

Next, I need to thank my critique partners, Renee Carlino and Amanda Maxlyn. Thank you both for helping me fix up Fix Her Up.

I also need to thank my early readers. Christine, Alisa, Kara, Ashley, Brenda, Nasha, Jennifer, Kimberly and Emma, I'm so lucky you guys are part of my crew.

Thank you to Jennifer Van Wyk for being my fantastic editor, Vanessa Brown for her excellent proof reading skills, Hang Le for designing this amazing cover, and Tami with Integrity Formatting for making my words look this good.

Lastly, a special thank you to every reader and blog who has read and shared my books. Your support means so much to me.

Thank you.

ABOUT THE AUTHOR

New York Times and USA Today bestselling romance author. She was born and raised in Alexandria, Virginia. Supporting her all the way are her husband, three sometimes-adorable children, a mischievous black cat, and their nine-pound attack Yorkie.

She loves to hear from her readers!
info@careyheywood.com

CPSIA information can be obtained
at www.ICGtesting.com
Printed in the USA
BVHW042139301121
622935BV00014B/855